Long Day
Monday

PETER TURNBULL

Long Day Monday

A Glasgow P Division procedural

St. Martin's Press
New York

FM
TURN

Library of Congress Cataloging-in-Publication Data

Turnbull, Peter.
    Long day Monday / Peter Turnbull.
        p.   cm.
    ISBN 0-312-08837-X
    I. Title.
PR6070.U68L66   1993
823′.914—dc20   92-43183
                                                      CIP

First published in Great Britain by HarperCollins Publishers.

First U.S. Edition: March 1993
10 9 8 7 6 5 4 3 2 1

Dedicated to
L.C.B.

Long Day
Monday

CHAPTER 1

In later years, in years of comfortable retirement, Ray Sussock would look upon the case as being perhaps the most satisfying of his career. He began with the case and he was there at the conclusion twenty-five years later, just prior to the conclusion of his own career. It would, though, be many months, if not years, before the sense of satisfaction, the sense of neatly rounding off, would settle in. At the time he found it harrowing, especially when the realization came. When the realization came he had woken up.

Screaming.

The man again noticed the car. He had first noticed it the day previous. There was nothing exceptional about it; nothing at all remarkable, nothing at all to distinguish it from many similar cars, nothing, like accident damage, to indicate its recent history. It was a Ford Escort, two years old and of Glasgow, by its plates, but more especially by the dealer's label still in the rear window. It was parked neatly on the grass verge, off the road, and the roads were narrow in these parts; it was easy to block the red roads of Lanarkshire. But the Ford, of a green not dissimilar to the shade of the grass on which it was stationed and which allowed it to blend into the scene, was neatly parked off the road, on the verge, close to the beginning of the avenue of lime trees now, in mid July, in full foliage. The trees lined the road, closely planted, and driving between them in mid-summer was akin to driving through a tunnel. The limes were a local landmark, loved by the people who lived near them and who kept their existence a jealously guarded secret. Coach trips had been known to make detours to view less than the avenue of limes near Carluke, Lanarkshire.

At the nearside of the car was the entrance to the driveway leading to Coles Wood Farm. Beyond the car was a fence of aged wire and rotting uprights, and beyond that was a field of lush pasture, and beyond that a second similar field but of higher elevation, and beyond that was rough grazing, then the hills, and beyond the hills the wilderness which stretched forty miles to the suburbs of Edinburgh. A dangerous, unforgiving place in winter.

At the far side of the road the ground fell into a meadow and beyond the meadow was the Clyde, not yet the murky, magnificent Clyde of the cranes and shipyard, nor the deepwater estuary scurrying south round the Tail of the Bank, but at that point a pleasant, rippling trout stream, about twenty feet wide, idyllically bounded by weeping willows amid which swallows swooped and darted. Beyond the Clyde were fields, and beyond the fields, some two miles distant, was the thundering A74; the 'big road', the 'trapdoor' route to England. By far the quickest way to leave Glasgow for England by car: open the trapdoor and fall south. It takes two hours. But here, midday, in deepest Lanarkshire, all was silent save for the uneven tickover of the Land-Rover engine, the occasional lowing of the Herefords, and the singing of the birds.

The man considered the car. Foreign. Foreign in the sense that it did not belong to the locality. And it had not been moved in the thirty-plus hours since he had first noticed it. He slipped the Land-Rover into first gear and drove into the entrance to Coles Wood Farm. He reached the farm buildings, parked the vehicle in the centre of the yard and entered the house. He didn't acknowledge his wife and she didn't acknowledge him. The smell of boiling vegetables filled the kitchen, the windows were

steamed up. The man moved with slow deliberate movements, in his own time, at his own pace. He was dressed
in a blue boilersuit, and black wellington boots splattered
in a green slime which dripped liberally on the vinyl. He
crossed the kitchen floor and picked the 'phone up.

'John McWilliams,' he said, after the preliminaries,
'Coles Wood Farm, Lanarkshire . . . near Carluke . . . I'd
like to report a car . . . at the entrance to my farm, it's been
there two days now. Yes, I wrote it down this morning . . .'
He rummaged in his pocket and pulled out a creased piece
of paper. He read out the registration. '. . . About an
hour.' He glanced up at the clock on the wall, a cheap
plastic clock, a white surround with black numerals and
hands, with a white wire running from it over the yellow-
painted plaster wall. He replaced the 'phone and sat at
the table, metal legs with a red formica top, and waited
as his thin wife laid a heaped meal before him. This
done, she dutifully withdrew to allow him to eat in peace.
John McWilliams grappled with the knife and fork with
widely extended elbows and ate in peace, with jerky
stabbing movements.

He completed his meal, tossed the knife and fork contemptuously on the plate and left the kitchen, and the
house. He clambered into the cab of the Land-Rover and
drove back to the entrance of the driveway, where he halted
the vehicle. He stepped out of the cab and leaned against
it, smoking a cigarette.

Not a sound now. The birds were quiet; the cattle were
sitting contentedly. He shook his head. No, no, he couldn't
live in the city, he was certain. He'd been there once or
twice, he wouldn't willingly go again, even if she yearned
to go back. His place was in the country and if his place
was here, so was hers. She knew what she was coming
to; she had visited, stayed overnight once and she'd been
happy enough to leave the tenements ten years ago. Can't

change her mind like that. Even if they weren't speaking any more, so what? They'd stopped doing anything else a long time ago . . . She'd made her bed, she had to lie on it.

McWilliams's thoughts were interrupted by the sound of a car approaching through the limes. He tossed the cigarette down. He knew that it was the police before he saw the car. He walked to the end of the drive.

Piper and Hamilton rode together, crewing Tango Delta Foxtrot which, under the luminous yellow flash on the sides, and the twin bubbles on the roof, was a top-of-the-range Granada, maintained in as near perfect condition as possible and quite content to be driven at 130 m.p.h. if and when necessary. Right then it was inching along at 5 m.p.h. with both Hamilton and Piper enjoying the unexpected pleasure of driving through a tunnel of limes in full foliage. Hamilton had recently been transferred to cars; usually a beat man, now he was in cars, and he found it a more comfortable existence; the action rapid. When it moved it moved like a rocket, it had a more thinking-on-one's-feet aspect, a more rapid response aspect, than he had found in the slower-moving life of a beat cop. He liked the excitement of cars, but missed the immediacy, the being in touch with the streets, the people, of a beat man's existence. Hamilton was finding his feet in cars, he was a slow-thinking man, slow-moving, methodical and thorough; not a man with brains that could set the heather on fire, but seen by his senior colleagues as being the solid leave-no-stone-unturned cop that is the backbone of the police force. A good man to have on the team. A very good man. He looked ahead and saw a figure in a boilersuit walk to the edge of the road and raise his hand.

'There,' said Hamilton.

'I've got him,' Piper replied testily, a little annoyed by Hamilton's observation which he thought needless and obvious. Piper drove slowly past the Escort and pulled half off the narrow road, riding Tango Delta Foxtrot up on to the grass verge and to the far side of the entrance to the farm. He and Hamilton left the car, putting on their caps as they did so.

McWilliams nodded to the Ford Escort, scowling, and Piper, more experienced than Hamilton, quicker-thinking, took an instant dislike to the man. Not a great dislike, but a nagging annoying dislike. He saw McWilliams as a dour hill farmer, and one who was struggling, the tear low down in his wellington boot which would allow water to seep in and the battered thirty-year-old series two Land-Rover he drove told him that. Piper, in serge trousers, crisp white shirt and black clip-on tie, walked towards McWilliams and saw him further as a man of little personality, little 'give' of himself, a detached personality and cold eyes, as blue as the vast sky above and behind him, but cold, cold, cold. A man, thought Piper, of little imagination, a man of things in their place and nowhere else.

'That's the car.' McWilliams spoke grudgingly, unnecessarily, letting it be known that he resented the interruption in his daily routine.

'How long has it been here?' Piper took his notebook from his shirt pocket.

'Two days. This is the second day. I first noticed it yesterday morning.'

Piper wrote in his notebook.

'You'll not be needing me any more.'

'If you'll stay a little longer, sir.' Piper spoke with polite insistence and without eye contact with McWilliams.

'Why?'

'If you'll remain here, sir.'

'Is it a stolen vehicle?' McWilliams changed his tack.

'Aye. From the grounds of Yorkhill Hospital on Tuesday night.' Piper fed McWilliams a little harmless information and glanced at the car. He thought it odd that the car was not abandoned like most stolen vehicles, but neatly parked, and with consideration too. Not just at the side of the road but, given the width of the road, it had been thoughtfully removed from the carriageway and parked on the verge. The doors had been locked and there was no apparent damage; even the radio had been left untouched.

McWilliams moved grumpily to the fence, leant on it and looked out across the pasture.

And who, Piper pondered, who would steal a car in Glasgow, drive it some twenty miles out of the city and then leave it neatly parked? He glanced about him. Fields and hills, there could only be about three houses in the immediate vicinity and none of them would soil their own nests by stealing a car, driving it home and leaving it outside the front gate, even if the gate was a mile from the home itself. It would be akin to a city dweller stealing a car and leaving it parked in his driveway.

Hamilton joined Piper. 'They're making contact with the owner. It'll be some time before he can recover the vehicle . . .'

But Piper wasn't listening to Hamilton. Piper was looking at McWilliams. Piper was looking at McWilliams because McWilliams was looking at him. McWilliams wasn't looking at Piper, he was staring him. Piper had felt affronted, he had felt affronted that a man, any man, should stare at him like that: a constant unrelenting eye-fixing stare. The sort of stare which says, You don't exist, but I'm going to stare at you anyhow. Out of uniform it would be bad enough; in uniform it was inexcusable, a direct challenge to the authority of the police. Then, suddenly, as if gaining an insight into the taciturn ways of the hill farmer, Piper realized that McWilliams wasn't staring at him; he was communicating with him, and he was communicating a message which read, 'Something is amiss, something bad, I think you should come and see this.' Piper left Hamilton without speaking and, falling in with the ways of non-verbal communication of the people of the land of the red roads, he walked up the verge and stood beside McWilliams. The man turned towards the field, and nodded to the immediate foreground.

A mound of earth, freshly dug, five feet long, two feet wide.

'Wasn't there three days ago,' said McWilliams.

'Got a spade?'

'Back of the Land-Rover.' Said in an if-you-want-it-you-fetch-it—sir, voice. Piper did so. Battered well-used spade in hand, he vaulted the fence and began to dig the freshly turned soil. He went down six inches.

A hand. Human; female from its size and rings.

He covered it again.

'Get on the radio,' Piper called to Hamilton as he drove the spade into the ground beside the body, as if to provide a marker. 'Tell them it's a Code 21.'

Ray Sussock had been a cop for most of his working life. He'd been a butcher's boy, he'd tended flowerbeds in a cemetery, he'd worked in the shipyards, he'd been on the dole, he'd worked in an office, he'd done his National Service in the RAF. He had enjoyed National Service, and had been unable to settle into the routine of civilian jobs following his two years in blue. He joined the police when in his mid-twenties. Now he was close to retirement and in that time, in excess of thirty years' service, he had risen from the rank of constable to that of detective-sergeant. Often, in moments of private recrimination, he felt that he had been given the promotion because of length of service

and little else, certainly not merit, certainly not for passing
the sergeants' exams. He hadn't sat any. But after fifteen
years in the CID the promotion had come suddenly and
unannounced. The job he did didn't seem to change
appreciably, but he had a grander title, a modest increase
in salary, he could look forward to a better pension, and
most valued of all, he had an office to himself. He had
personal space. A door which he could open and shut as
the fancy took him.

He had always worked shifts, and still did. The day shift
until 14.00 hours, the back shift until 22.00, the night shift
until 06.00, and like all officers he had his shift card, which
rotated through a four-week cycle with which he could cal-
culate the shift he'd be working on any given day in the
future, any number of years in the future, because the four-
week rotation rotated endlessly, unstoppably, taking no
heed of Christmastide, Easter or Bank holidays. Except that
in his case, in the late afternoon of his life, he had ceased
calculating his shifts for more than a few months in
advance. He could scent retirement, well earned and overdue. Like any cop, once he had adjusted to working shifts
he found that he had a strong preference for shift work. He
worked them one shift at a time until the days off, and then
he wasted the days off, never seeming to do half the things
he had planned to do before the shifts started again. That's
how it had gone on, week to week, month to month, season
to season, year to year. He doubted now that he could
adjust to a nine-to-five routine. When he was younger he
resented having to work Saturday nights, and now in his
late middle years he longed for peaceful Sundays at home;
but more than that he longed for a peaceful home to have
Sundays in. That aside, he felt something not dissimilar to
privilege in being out of step with society, having free time
midweek, queueless roads and shops, uncrowded pubs, a
gentler feel to each midweek day if he was on a rest day.

And he enjoyed the job, shifts or no shifts, which took him out of doors, away from the prejudice and pettiness of the office routine, like the office he had once worked in when morning coffee and afternoon tea were taken, certainly, but only upon the instruction of the supervisor whose whims meant that the breaks took place within a 'window' as vast as ninety minutes. But he was just seventeen then and still learning. Never again, locked in an office for eight hours a day with two dozen woodenheads and no escape. Never again. Shifts were for him; even at his age, he could cope with shifts better than he could cope with the nine-to-five.

But there were drawbacks, perhaps the most agonizing being the rule similar to the rule in the television quiz game, 'You've started, so you can finish,' though in the police it is, 'You've started, so you must finish.' A cop was not guaranteed freedom upon the time expiry of his shift. If a cop picks up a job half an hour before the end of his shift he'll finish it—eight hours later. Sussock glanced at the clock on the wall above the battered grey Scottish Office issue metal filing cabinet. 13.10. Fifty minutes to go. It hadn't been a bad shift, midweek day shift, nothing major, nothing to get his teeth into, nothing that had dominated the shift; no 'big one'. There had been boys on the run from a List D school, hanging about the bus station and found to be in possession of controlled drugs, which had been largely handled by the uniformed branch who had informed Sussock as a courtesy. There had been a mugging in a peripheral scheme, a young woman had had her handbag stolen and her money had been taken: 'Two weeks' social security, so it was.' Or had she? Sussock found her too much in control, too full of indignation, to be a victim of a crime. She gave a hazy description of 'a man about twenty, in denims' who had pushed her to the ground and had run away with her handbag, and money. The incident had happened in broad daylight in the street but no witness had come forward. Sussock had been deeply suspicious, a suspicion largely confirmed when the woman had asked for a 'pink slip'. 'The social won't replace the money, but, unless I have a pink slip, but.'

But he had given her a pink slip anyway, but: theft notified to the police, amount lost, date and time. He could not disprove her story any more than he could prove it and what the hell, people just can't live on the amount social security pays out anyway, people on social security need to moonlight or pull shots like reporting non-existent crimes to boost their income survival level. Need breeds remarkable ingenuity.

A boy had been reported missing by his distraught mother, just ten years old. Details had been taken, description faxed to every police station in Strathclyde. The family home had been searched, every nook and cranny from the basement to rafter in front of a disbelieving and distressed mother and her comforting neighbour.

'It's nothing to be embarrassed or offended about, madam,' Sussock had said calmly, gently: there was no need to add to her distress. 'It's routine. In a case like this we have to cover every possibility, check the obvious first. We are not accusing you or pointing the finger of blame. He might be hiding: that's happened before.'

'Or in case his body's been hidden,' the woman sobbed. 'That's what you're saying. In case he's been done away with. Why don't you dig the garden while you're at it?'

The Alsatian in the modest rear garden was in fact a sniffer dog and was at that time sitting contentedly on the lawn awaiting the next command from his handler. The woman had assumed the Alsatian to be a police dog and nothing more: Sussock felt disinclined to disabuse her of that notion. 'It's just routine,' he had said again, and the woman turned and buried her head in her neighbour's shoulder.

It *was* just routine at this stage, but Sussock had put his years in, he was an experienced cop, he had expertise if he wasn't an expert. He had developed a 'nose' for a 'nasty one' and he didn't like the smell of this one, not at all. A middle-class area of Glasgow, a tree-lined avenue, 'sought-after family home in a stonebuilt terrace' as the estate agents would say, inhabited by professional people, responsible people, as in this home: mother a teacher, father a university teacher presently on a lecture tour of the States. This was the sort of neighbourhood where children are well brought up, go where they are allowed to go and nowhere else, come home on time and not a minute later, and who always say 'no' to strangers—say 'no' and run away, especially if he's in a car. No, he didn't like this one at all. Not at all.

At 14.30 he still didn't like that one. He had allocated the case to Elka Willems who had already done a good job of drafting a missing persons poster. He had approved it and sent it to the printers, who now only waited for the word 'go' before running off two hundred copies in the first instance, but he had privately envisaged many more copies being needed; in fact, he had rapidly envisaged a national coverage for this one, every police station, large and small, every railway station, every bus station, every public library, and the London Underground system as well. Sussock just had this feeling, a gut-wrenching certainty that Tim Moore of Broomhill would not come running home bubbling an apology. Indeed, he had a gut-wrenching feeling of certainty that Tim Moore would not be coming home at all. But it was still officially a missing person, a missing child, not three hours old, a child who had not returned home for lunch and still had not returned by mid-afternoon. It was too early to panic, too early to organize a house-to-house, too early to sweep local open country, gap sites, waste ground, with troops and civilian volunteers. Sussock had tried to comfort himself. He had had similar gut feelings before which had in the event proved groundless. He'd been proved wrong before. He'd also been proved right before. At that moment the file on Tim Moore, aged ten, was thin and crisp and new, a top sheet providing basic information—name, numbers, address—and so far a single handwritten continuation sheet recording the visit to the Moore household and the drawing up of the missing person poster. It also contained a photograph of Tim, a smiling boy with golden hair and a blue sweater taken in Saltcoats earlier this year. It looks sunny but the wind was cold. 'He'd just had his first Knickerbocker Glory in Nardini's. In fact his first ever, not just his first in . . .' but the rest had been lost in a flood of tears.

There had been one good solid-as-a-rock collar during the day: late in the morning a young man had been observed breaking into a car with intent to steal. He had come quietly, a practised felon who seemed to know when the game was up. A visit to his home had revealed a backyard strewn with parts from twenty or thirty cars, ready to be sold as bolt-on spare parts, everything from engine blocks and gearboxes to wing mirrors. Inside the house had been a similar treasure trove of hi-fi's, fascias, upholstery. Two uniformed officers were still there drawing up an inventory. The man was in the cells, Pringle sweater and slacks, jawing frantically, jawing with his solicitor, looking for a plea bargain.

And that was it. Montgomerie on the graveyard shift had handed over to him at 06.00, bleary-eyed and stubbled, and hadn't passed any work on, and he looked like keeping his end up with Richard King who was to take over from him at 14.00. The CID officers took a sense of pride in not handing work on to each other, but 'cleared their shift' if they could. The case of Tim Moore was the only worrying one, and deeply worrying at that, but at this stage all that could be done had been done.

No. No, it hadn't.

One thing had not been done.

Sussock reached forward and picked up the 'phone on his desk. He dialled 9 for an outside line and then a seven figure number. A gruff male voice said 'Yes?' after the 'phone had rung once and then been picked up.

'Taxi Owners' Association?' asked Sussock.

'TOA. Aye.'

'Police.'

'Aye?'

'We have a missing child.'

'Aye.' But in a concerned, interested tone.

'Could you circulate the description for us, please?'

'Aye.'

'Ten years old, male,' said Sussock, opening the file, 'blond hair, dressed in a shell suit, red and white shell suit. Called Tim. Last seen at home address in the West End of Glasgow, but could be anywhere.'

The TOA controller read the description back.

'That's it,' said Sussock. 'If you'd put it out on the air as soon as you like. We'll get posters to you for your garages and control rooms as soon as we print them.'

'Will do, sir.'

'Appreciate it.' Sussock put the 'phone down and in the Moore file added to the continuation sheet: '13.10, 'phoned TOA, gave description to be circulated over the radio.'

Glasgow is a taxi-minded city, the 'fast blacks', the London-style cabs, swarm across the city from the intimacy of the grid system at her centre to the anonymous dull expanse of the peripheral schemes, and the taxi-drivers have evolved as the unnoticed eyes of the police. They have often—more out of excitement than public duty—assisted in police chases (but better doing it than being uninterested), they have reported crimes in progress over the short wave, rushed victims to hospital. Equally, the taxi-drivers have to survive and have kept quiet when advised to do so. A cab hailed in Castlemilk by three guys in long coats was directed to Dennistoun. Two guys left the cab and went up a close taking sawn-offs from under their coats while the third guy stays in the cab, coolly drawing on a nail and says equally coolly, 'Keep the motor running, Jim,' and 'My mates come back, take us to "the milk" and drop us.' Then the driver heard four distinct shotgun blasts from inside the close, the two guys came back hurriedly, but not running, weapons concealed, climbed into the cab. The driver swung the vehicle and drove south of the water, back to 'the milk'. In 'the milk' he stopped close to where he had picked up the three hardcases and they left the cab. Two walked away without looking back, but the third, the one who'd stopped in the cab while the turn was going down, stood by the cab door and stared into the face of the driver and said, 'I've clocked you, I've clocked the number of this cab—keep it shut,' then he bunged the driver a wedge of more than ten times the fare. Later that night the driver hears of a double murder in Dennistoun, believed to be gangland and drug-related. Police, and the Radio Clyde bulletins, are appealing for witnesses. But the driver, sensibly, had kept it shut.

Sussock had heard about the incident years after it had happened and attached no blame to the driver. What person could? But this was different, a missing child. The taxi-drivers compose an unofficial community watch and just like the police they could maintain a watch around the clock: twenty-four-hour monitoring.

Tim Moore was the only 'live' case he had to hand over to Richard King. King couldn't complain and wouldn't, he'd be home on time, a fine afternoon . . .

His telephone rang. He picked it up. '295, Sussock.'

'Switchboard, sir,' said a young, keen as mustard, female voice. 'Tango Delta Foxtrot has just requested CID attendance at the locus of a stolen vehicle.'

'Why?' Sussock sighed before he knew he was speaking. 'Just notify the owner and get him to recover it . . .'

'They reported a Code 21, sir.'

Sussock's heart hit the floor. 'A murder,' he said.

'CID attendance requested, sir,' the voice repeated with an added note of urgency.

It was all right for her, Sussock reflected bitterly, she'd be off the switchboard on time, switchboard and clerical staff didn't ever . . .

'All right.' He put the 'phone down. Could he get out of it? It was less than an hour to lowsing time, the team comes and goes with each other, he could do nothing and sit on the request for fifty minutes and appeal to Richard King's better nature, but that would look too bad, fifty minutes and nothing to show for it, and he knew what Richard's response would be: 'Oh, come on, Sarge, it didn't come in at 13.50, it came in at 13.10. In fact, it came in earlier and just changed to a Code 21 at 13.10, the case is two hours old,' and: 'You're right, I don't like the smell of the Tim Moore case. Even if it is brand new it has an old and familiarly unpleasant odour. We're into the white nights, I've got daylight until 22.30, I'd like to sweep local open areas, start looking at the disused railway tunnels . . . I think I'd like to start on it, not drag my feet, and I can't do two major investigations, haven't the resources . . . and you know the rules. And Tango Delta Foxtrot wouldn't take kindly to being kept fifty minutes longer than necessary . . .'

Sussock knew fine well what the incoming constable would say. And he'd be right to say it. It had for Sussock just been a passing fancy, a fantasy that he indulged in briefly for a second or two. It had flooded into his mind and it had lingered there, he had toyed with it, wondering how he could make it work and finally accepting that he couldn't, not in any way that he could square with his conscience. He then reached forward and picked up the 'phone on his desk. He dialled a two-figure internal number which was answered promptly by the young, keen as mustard, female operator who would be home on time. 'Switchboard.'

'Sussock,' he said. 'Inform Tango Delta Foxtrot that I'll be with them asap. ETA thirty minutes from now.'

'Very good, sir.'

He replaced the telephone receiver and stood, wearily. He walked to the hatstand and picked up his light summer coat which had long since lost its shape and which now hung from him like a sack, and he also plucked from a hook a long since fashionable summer hat. He walked out of his office and into the CID corridor.

A detached observer would have noted a certain resignation in his step, and a weariness across his eyes which were set deep in his craggy life- and weather-beaten features.

'Don't like it here. I want to go now.'

'Soon. Not yet. Your mother will collect you. Play with the rabbits. I told you I'd show you some rabbits. Stop crying. I'm going now. I'll leave the light on.'

The door closed. The key turned.

She went down the long dark corridor. She went into the huge heavily and densely furnished room which could never be heated, even in summer. It always had a chill about it. It always had. She sat in the deep armchair and felt two old springs giving under her weight. She pondered the threadbare carpet, the old paintings in heavy frames, the moth-eaten curtains, the old plants in copper pots. She had grown up in this house, moved from this house, assumed ownership when they had died, grown old here.

Murdered here.

Been taken away from here.

Murdered here again.

And again and again.

Now she had another little boy. He was about as old as the first one. All those years ago.

Strange how things seemed to come full circle. After those young women it was a child now. A boy. Again.

'Just him and me in this huge flat, must be the only flat in the street which is still one-family occupancy. Family, that's rich, just me and my guest, when I have one.' The woman continued to ponder. All six rooms and the walk-in cupboard, the guest room, the room that had kept the guests over the years. Made for the job, the guests could scream and shout until they grew hoarse. The walls backed on to the other rooms in the flat or back court where only cats and city foxes went these days. The ceiling was twenty feet above, and the floor was the floor, nothing underneath at all. Except the clay and they'd be in that soon enough.

She thought again about the boy, talked to him on impulse walking down the street, so angelic, so appealing, the blond hair, the smile like a sunburst, so she stopped the car and asked him if he wanted to see some rabbits?

Maybe she had wanted a child again. Maybe that's why she had done it. She wanted a child. Something deep within her craved for a child. She'd keep him a day or two, but then she'd have to serve him as she had the others. If she let him go he'd only talk and then they'd take her away again to the place of white huts and wire on the hills near where the railway line divides, near where the trains from England split into two, front half for Glasgow, rear half for Edinburgh. Then, after years and years had come and gone, they'd put her in a van and driven her to a place of rambling

brick next to another railway line, the one between Edinburgh and Glasgow, where she'd knitted and watched the
trains thunder by as if travelling across the fields, where
she'd been surrounded by females in dressing-gowns.

They never checked the flat. Each time they'd taken her
away they'd never checked the flat. They just made sure
the windows were closed, the gas and electricity turned off
and the front door locked. They didn't check the rooms,
especially the locked one, and the last time they took her
away she had a guest, weak from thirst and starvation, too
weak to cry out or scratch on the door, and when she
returned after shock treatment and drug therapy, it was
to a semi-mummified corpse. It had been a day's job to
dismember the body and put it into bin liners; easier than
a fresh corpse, though; the fluids had solidified. She tossed
a bin liner into a skip here, another into a skip there. The
rest she took up to the council dump at Dawnsholme and
a kindly man helped her lever it up into the huge container
to be taken away for incineration.

The real problem had been the smell, took a week to get
rid of the smell, couldn't be smothered with aerosol, she
had had to get close in on her hands and knees and scrub
the walk-in cupboard with bleach and open the nearest
windows, buy incense from the craft shop on Great Western
Road and burn it continually. The smell was always a problem; sound may well travel downwards in tenements, but
smells rise. The people in the flat above were young,
exuberant, they polluted her flat with their noise, loud
music, stamping feet and squeaky bedsprings. They got her
smells. The smell could have been awkward but these old
tenements were not just built, they were solidly built. Her
ceiling might well have been their floor, but the two were
separated by eighteen inches of grit filling. It had kept the
odour of rotting flesh contained until she had been deemed
fit and sane and able to return to the community.

She turned and gazed at her reflection in the mirror. Heavy features, heavy frame, short dark hair, silver tufts here and there, matched by her dark jacket. Fit and strong. Good for her years.

She'd keep the boy for a few days. Maybe till early next week. He probably wouldn't survive as long as an adult anyway.

'Just seemed odd, right from the start, Sarge,' said Piper. 'It just didn't look right. I mean, stolen cars are abandoned, doors left unlocked, open even, they're not locked and neatly parked. Most of the time they're vandalized; this one's been cared for.'

'Who reported it?' Sussock felt he had to say something. Piper, junior in both years and rank, and in uniform, seemed to be more on the ball than he. Sussock felt a certain challenge to his authority.

'This gentleman here, sir.' Piper nodded to McWilliams, who stood against his Land-Rover, perspiring gently in the sun. Sussock glanced at McWilliams, a stocky man, dour of expression, whose one concession to the heat seemed to have been to roll his overall sleeves up above his elbows. He took his eyes from McWilliams and looked lovingly about him, at the fields and the blue hills, filling his lungs with sweet country air as he did so. It was not often that his job took him out of the city: not often that he could breathe so freely. He suffered badly from bronchitis and the thin air of the Scottish winters was difficult for him, and the thicker exhaust-heavy air of the city summers was only a little easier, a brief respite, but here in the country, in the summer with the trees in full foliage, the sweet Clyde flowing softly through a meadow, it was a rare opportunity for him to fill his lungs. He no longer begrudged this particular piece of overtime, this piece of 'you've started, so you must finish'.

'And it was while we were here, Sarge, that Mr Mc-
Williams drew our attention to the grave.'

'The grave?' Sussock brushed a troublesome fly from in
front of his eyes.

'For want of a better word, Sarge. It's in the field. Just
here.'

'Wisnae there two days ago.' McWilliams spat on the
ground. 'Fresh dug.'

Sussock nodded. He thought McWilliams must be at the
very edge of earshot.

'I borrowed the gentleman's spade, sir,' Piper continued.
'Went down about ten inches. Came across an arm, I think.'

'You think.'

'What appears to be an arm.' Piper stuck rigidly to basic
training, never saying what he'd found/seen, but what he
appeared to have found/seen.

'An arm,' Sussock repeated.

'Human. Appears to be female from the rings on the
fingers. Still flesh-covered. No evidence of decomposition,
so far as I could detect. I covered it up and reported it.'

'Very good.' Sussock felt himself falling into a state of
numbness. What to do, what to do? People looking at him.
He began to wish himself far away. He shook himself into
sensibility. 'Right . . . we need assistance . . . The first thing
to do is to cordon off the area, the corner of the field,
say one hundred feet square, encompassing the grave . . .
Careful where you tread. Don't have to tell you not to touch
anything.'

Piper turned and walked briskly to the boot of Tango
Delta Foxtrot and took a coil of blue and white tape, three
inches thick, from the boot. He climbed the fence and
stepped into the field and, taking McWilliams's spade from
beside the mound of freshly turned soil, he carried it away
from the grave to a point a hundred feet in the field from the
road and one hundred feet from the track to McWilliams's

farmhouse and slung the tape from the fence to the spade to the fence, thus forming a cordoned-off area one hundred feet square, as requested by DS Sussock, senior officer at the locus. As he was delineating the square, Hamilton was also acting on the instructions of DS Sussock, sitting in Tango Delta Foxtrot and speaking on the radio, passing on Sergeant Sussock's request for a pathologist, please, extra men for a search, bags and tags, scene of crimes officer, car to be collected for forensic examination.

Sussock approached McWilliams. 'If you didn't see anything, sir, perhaps you might have heard something?'

'No.' McWilliams didn't look at Sussock, but kept his eyes on his property, his spade presently being tied up with fancy blue and white ribbon. 'When do I get my spade back?'

'When we've finished with it, sir. All in good time.'

'I wish I'd never reported the car. I'm losing a good working afternoon.'

'We'd have spoken to you anyway. I assume this is your field?'

'Aye.'

'Well, in that case we'd certainly have been taking up some of your time anyway,' Sussock growled. He was feeling happier now. Things were more under control, his control. 'Where is your house?'

McWilliams tossed his head contemptuously over his shoulder in the direction of the drive, but Sussock could only see a deeply rutted path driving low between two elevated fields towards a wood on the skyline, breaking the line between the fields and the hills. He was uncertain whether McWilliams's evident contempt was towards the police for invading his time and property or for his house, still unseen.

'Between the trees,' said McWilliams, by means of explanation. Sussock noted a ruddy complexion and the breath of a serious drinker. 'We don't see much of night and nobody sees much of us. I like it that way.'

'Whose "we"?'

'Me and the wife. She's not a bad woman, she does her duty most of the time.'

'We'll need to talk to her.'

'Why?'

'In case she saw something.'

'She didn't.'

'How do you know?'

'She didn't see anything. Take it from me, Jim. She saw nothing. And I mean nothing.'

A swallow swooped low overhead, a zephyr rustled the branches of the limes and then they were still once again. A canary-yellow car, mud-caked, drove along the road, slowed at the presence of police activity but didn't stop. McWilliams raised his hand in greeting and the driver nodded in response.

'My neighbour,' explained McWilliams, 'Henry Abbott. He has the next farm. He's an owner. I'm a tenant. It'd make some difference if I owned my farm. I make a good income and then send a fair portion of it twice a year to a company in Perth. The wife, she saw nothing.'

'She'll have to tell us that.'

'I'll need to be there.'

'No, you won't.'

McWilliams stiffened, controlling himself. He clenched his hands into two huge fists and then relaxed.

'Just you and Mrs McWilliams at home, then?'

'Why?'

'Just a question.'

'Aye,' McWilliams replied after a pause. Sussock glanced at his watch. 13.58. Two minutes to knocking-off time.

Some hope. Some wild hope, old Sussock. This is the real world and you live in it, here and nowhere else. He turned and glanced at the tape suspended over the grass. He glanced at the mound of freshly turned soil. But at least he lived.

He wanted the light to go out.

The naked bulb hurt his eyes.

He didn't like rabbits, soft fluffy toys. Girls' toys. He lay down and used one as a pillow.

He didn't like the woman, she smiled below cold eyes.

Her mouth smiled but her eye devoured him. He could only see one eye: she held her hand over the other. He had only ever seen one eye, even on the first day she had worn a patch. He found himself referring to her as One-Eye.

CHAPTER 2

Thursday, 14.00–15.40 hours

Dr Reynolds ran his silver Volvo estate up on to the high, grassed bank, the wide tyres, high ground clearance and stiff suspension making easy work of the manœuvre, a manœuvre which would be beyond the capacity of many makes of motorcar. He would open the sun roof to allow the interior of the car to 'breathe' in his absence. It was, he felt, a wise precaution on a day like this, hot and still. He left the vehicle and walked towards Sergeant Sussock and surveyed the scene as he walked: a lane bounded by trees, thus forming an avenue, a low meadow to his left and to the left of the road, beyond which the smooth clear, clean waters of the Clyde glinted in the sun, willows overhanging, a kingfisher darting. To his right and to the right of the red lane were the police vehicles, Sergeant Sussock's car, a second car and a Land-Rover at the end of a track which

thrust into the field. A man slouched against the Land-
Rover. One corner of the field seemed to have been
cordoned off by a police tape—white and blue—which for
the most part hung limp and then occasionally, for a
second, would flutter as it was tugged gently by a breeze.
Beyond the tape was the green of the pasture and standing
on the pasture were police officers, white shirts and black
trousers, about ten, thought Reynolds, all walking in a line
across the pasture, searching the ground, forcing the cattle
to inch away in front of them. Beyond the line of police
officers was the blue of the distant hills and beyond that
the lighter blue of the canopy of the sky with just a wisp of
white cloud high and to westward.

Sussock stepped towards Reynolds and tugged the brim
of an imaginary hat. 'Good afternoon, sir.'

The tall, silver-haired pathologist smiled and mumbled
an excuse for his late arrival. The directions he had been
given were excellent, but he had taken the wrong turning
after Carluke. So sorry.

'No problem, sir.' Sussock smiled. 'It's over here, sir.'
He noted again, as often he had noticed in the past, how
Reynolds's hair matched perfectly the silver of his car. But
Sussock did not think it was vanity on the part of Reynolds;
the pathologist was not a man to be vain; it would be
coincidence and nothing more. Dr Reynolds, in Sussock's
view, would probably not have noticed the colour match.

Reynolds followed Sussock as the police officer led him
between the stolen car and the police minibus to the edge
of the field and he immediately saw the grave half opened.

'All right,' he said, more to himself than to anyone else,
'can we start digging, please?' He clambered over the wire
at the edge of the field as Sussock motioned to two constables, who stood by with spades in their hands, to com-
mence digging. A third officer stood by with a screen, made
up of poles and an orange plastic sheet.

'Just uncover the corpse, please,' Reynolds addressed the constables as they began to remove the soil in as near vertical layers as possible, and then, turning to Sussock, 'I dare say you'd like to have the body photographed before it is removed, Sergeant?'

'Certainly would, sir. We have a scene of crime officer present.'

'Right, then, let's be methodical. If nothing else, let's be methodical, above all let's be methodical. I had expected your senior to be present, Sergeant, not that I have less than absolute faith in you as a professional, but it has always seemed to me that Fabian Donoghue tends to take a keen interest in this sort of thing; he always struck me as wanting to be present at the locus.'

'Day off, sir,' said Sussock, patiently waiting for Reynolds to finish his question. 'I mean he's taken a day's leave; a family wedding, I believe.'

'Good.' Reynolds nodded. 'A good day for it.' A pause: held. A different tone. 'Good man is Donoghue, a good chap.'

'Yes, sir,' said Sussock.

The two police officers stopped digging and stepped back, but their gaze was fixed downwards. Sussock saw that they were both shaken, the older man, all of twenty-eight or twenty-nine, looked as though he had been that way before, but the younger one, barely twenty, thought Sussock, had evidently come across a milestone in his career. Sussock saw his chest heave as he dropped the spade and walked away towards the centre of the field.

'Turn round, Constable,' Sussock called to him. 'Don't panic, hold it in your mouth till you get to the end of the field. And take your time, you've got all the time in the world. Breathe through your nose.'

The younger constable turned and walked to the edge of the field; over-controlled, over-concentrating, he climbed

the fence and stepped on to the track behind McWilliams's
Land-Rover. He leaned forward and vomited.

'Good man,' Sussock called, as the constable wiped his
mouth.

McWilliams watched the spectacle with a detached
smile, then turned and spat on the ground.

Reynolds and Sussock approached the grave and stood
in silence as they looked downwards. Youth and beauty in
a fœtal position in ten inches of soil. Eyes open. Mouth
open. A heavy rope ligature round the neck and stout stick
to tighten it.

'We'll photograph it now,' said Sussock, turning.

'Her.' Reynolds held a respect for the dead. 'Photograph
her.'

'I meant "it" as in the scene of the crime.' Sussock spoke
coldly. 'Sir.'

'Very well.'

'We'll photograph the scene and then erect the screen,
sir.' Reynolds turned and walked with Sussock away from
the grave, and as they did so they noticed the young constable spitting to clean his throat and then saw that his eyes
seemed caught by something, an object on the ground, not
visible to Reynolds and Sussock. He stooped to pick it up.

'Don't touch it,' Sussock yelled. He was still stung by
Reynolds's rebuke which might well have been born out of
a simple misunderstanding but had more or less created a
tension between the two men. 'Excuse me, sir,' he said and
walked across the field, climbed the fence and stood next
to the young constable.

A rabbit. A small furry toy. A child's toy, light blue. It
lay in the long grass which ran up the centre of the track,
a meridian of grass with deep ruts at either side which ran
from the lane to the farm house. The toy rabbit would have
been easily missed.

'It's out of place,' said the constable. 'I mean, there's

nothing sinister about it, Sergeant, it just seems foreign to
the locus.'

Sussock nodded, impressed. The young man clearly had
the makings of a very good policeman.

'It hasn't been here long. It's not weathered. A young
child's toy, here in the middle of nowhere, and next to a
murder scene. It just doesn't add up and deliver.'

'Any children about here?' Sussock raised his voice sufficiently for it to carry to McWilliams who stood some
twenty feet distant.

'No.' Said finally, after a long authority-testing pause.

'Bag it and tag it, please,' said Sussock. The constable
turned and walked to the police minibus. Sussock remained
as if rooted to the spot. Something gnawed away at him.
Deep, deep in the recesses of his memory, like a smell
remembered but which could not be placed; a word which
had a significance which couldn't be recalled; a sound
which awakened misty, hazy memories. He was certain
that here, half on its side in the parched grass, the blue
toy, less than twelve inches long, had a real, strong
positive significance.

To his left a camera bulb flashed. Sussock was surprised
that a flash was needed on a day like this, but the scene of
crime officer knew his job and knew it well. The flash
brought Sussock's attention back to the matter in hand. He
left the track and walked towards the grave. The scene of
crime officer took five more photographs and then withdrew. The screen was erected around the grave and Dr
Reynolds, bag in hand, stepped inside the screen.

Elka Willems caught her breath. She hoped that the
woman did not hear her.

'And he's not with any friends, they'd have 'phoned to
tell us that he was with them, or they would have allowed
him to use the 'phone. And we have no relatives he could

be with; as I told you before, we're not Glaswegians, neither of us. We have relations in Stirling, they're the nearest— the nearest in terms of geography—but pretty distant in terms of kinship. Tom's family are Aberdonians. I am from the Western Isles, so no, Miss Willems, he hasn't gone to a friend or a relative.'

She was a brave woman. Elka Willems thought that she was a brave woman. A woman of less calibre would have been reduced to histrionics or worked herself up into a panic and gone running about the streets, but not Edwina Moore. She was bravely containing a flood of emotion while answering the policewoman's questions as lucidly and laconically as she could. Elka Willems thought her to be a woman of steel. Then she said it again: '. . . and how often, how often we have told him, drummed it into him, that he's not to go with a strange man. We've said to him, "If a strange man approaches you, then run away, and if he's in the car run in the opposite direction to the direction of the car."

This time Elka Willems made no sound. She nodded sympathetically but said to herself, 'Why men, why only men?' but hindsight with all its wisdom was, she thought, the last thing that Edwina Moore needed in the present situation. It would have been better to say 'strangers', Mrs Moore, Elka Willems's thoughts ran on as she allowed her gaze to sweep once again around the room. It was solidly and, she thought, tastefully decorated; not aggressive, not opulent, not of low-taste conspicuous consumption, but quiet, high quality, the room of people here to stay, of putting down roots and bringing up a family. It was the home of two successful professionals. Her gaze swept further, through the huge panes of glass which framed the front bay window and out on to the tree-lined suburban road; palatial terraced, and wide enough for Mercedes and

Saabs to park nose in to the kerb and still leave a passage
for cars in the centre.

'So what can we do?' Edwina Moore appealed to Elka
Willems.

'Nothing much more. In fact, nothing more.' Elka Willems spoke softly. Her job now was to retain contact with
the family, to offer emotional support, to call on the family,
to reassure them that the police had not forgotten Tim
Moore; that all that could be done was still being done; and
this is what we did today, and tomorrow we will be doing
this. Elka Willems might have told Mrs Moore that she
would continue to call alone, even hopefully bring good
news alone, but if she was seen approaching the house in
the company of another officer, if ever it was apparent that
the visit has been deemed a 'two-hander' . . .

'The photograph of Tim is being duplicated and missing
persons posters are being run off. They'll be posted in police
stations, bus and railway stations in the Glasgow area over
the next few days. If necessary, we'll extend it to national
coverage. The taxi-drivers have their eyes peeled. They've
come up with the goods in the past. A search . . .'

'A search?' There was a note of alarm in Edwina Moore's
voice.

'We have to prepare for every eventuality. Even the
worst.'

'I suppose. It's just that you don't like to entertain the
thought that he's out there somewhere. At least the
weather's good. He'll not get cold if the weather holds, it's
hot enough to survive without a top coat . . .' She paused,
collected her emotions, restrained them, breathing in
deeply, breathing out slowly. 'You never think that it could
happen to you,' she said, looking up at the ceiling. 'You
read of tragedies, children dying, being run down, and
you think: How awful for the parents, and then you get on
with your own rich, untraumatized, cup-runneth-over,

rewarding life. I mean, everything on your plate, a good and a successful husband, a lovely house, fabulous neighbours, lovely healthy little boy who went out to play for half an hour before lunch . . . and then an hour or so later your world has crashed . . . and you take a walk, go to the shops on the corner and you see people going about their business, cars and buses plying back and forth, and you think: "How dare they?" You think: "My little boy is missing and they're just carrying on as though nothing matters, as though nothing has happened . . ." it's like the world, life, is going on without us.'

'Is your husband coming back tomorrow?' Elka Willems asked after a respectful pause.

Edwina Moore nodded. 'He's cut short his lecture tour. He did so as soon as he heard the news. He's getting the first flight back. He's trying for a flight to Glasgow or Prestwick, but he'll take the first flight back to the UK.'

'It'll be good to have him home.'

'It will, it will. I wonder how we'll be in bed?'

Elka Willems's look hardened.

Edwina Moore saw the look of disapproval in Elka Willems's eyes and she managed a brief yet healthy smile. 'Don't misunderstand me, I'm not lamenting any loss of our sex life, I'm not bothered about that. What I mean is, that when things go well with us we lie close, in each other's arms. We might well disentangle during the night but we go to sleep like that. If things have been stressed, as when we have had a row, we lie apart, or one of us sleeps in the spare room. I wonder how we'll be tomorrow night, or the night after when Murdoch's back? We've never been this way before, we might cling to each other, we might be happier alone, carrying our own fears. I wonder how he'll feel . . . He'll not blame me?' A rush of panic.

'There's no blame that can be attached to you.' Elka Willems shook her head. She was severely dressed in white blouse and serge trousers, yet none the less, to Edwina Moore's eyes, stunningly attractive: high cheekbones and the blonde hair of her Nordic ancestors. She wore her hair in a bun, and about her slender neck a blue and white chequered cravat which fastened at the rear with Velcro and which would come away in the hands of any thug who might try to garotte her with it.

'I can't help but blame myself.' She looked down at the wall-to-wall Axminster which to Elka Willems seemed more worn than the rest of the décor and not quite gelling with the room, as if it had been left by the previous owner and 'lived with' by the present owners because the cost of its replacement was beyond their present means. But it was an Axminster, plenty of life in it yet.

'I want Murdoch's presence,' said Edwina Moore. 'I want my husband here, but I don't think that I could bear his touch.'

'He might feel the same.'

'I think he will. He's very strong. He's not cloying or weak, he'll keep his worries and his fears from me, he'll carry those himself.'

Elka Willems glanced at the carriage clock on the mantelpiece, a white face in a gold frame with three balls spinning round beneath the face, first clockwise, then anti-clockwise. It was 02.30 p.m. She didn't mind working on in a situation like this. In a situation like this the last thing any cop would be thinking of was the end of his or her shift. This was human need, raw and desperate, the sharp end of the business: tragedy.

Privately she thought how Tim Moore would be found. He'd be found smashed, a bag of fractured bones at the bottom of a mineshaft that no one knew had existed; or miles away, discovered by a farm hand engaged in hedging and ditching, naked, bruised massively about the neck, torn and blood-caked anus, blood in his mouth, eyes open; or he'd be found by a council refuse collector nonchalantly tossing black bin liners into the rear of the wagon, slowly uncovering the beaten and bloody remains of Tim Moore with a battered skull and semen traces in mouth and anus, from how many secretors? One, four, more than four? Or perhaps his body would never be found; such things happened. People just disappear as if into thin air. That possibility, the possibility that Edwina and Murdoch Moore would never find out what happened to Tim, their first and so far only child, was in Elka Willems's view far, far worse than knowing the full extent of the tragedy, especially as the days melted into weeks, and months into years. Elka Willems reached for her cap and caught Edwina Moore's mixed look of disappointment and acceptance of her leaving. She could not stay forever and now all useful purpose of her visit had been exhausted. There was no new information to relay, no more emotional stroking to be done. The police were there to provide a public service, maybe to lean on for a while, but not endlessly. At some point every victim, every bereaved person, has to pick themselves up and carry on. Nobody said it was an easy ride, and nobody gets out alive.

'I'll call tomorrow.' Elka Willems stood. Edwina Moore stood also. She was shorter than Elka Willems but had yet again given Elka Willems the impression of a tall woman, a woman whose legs were proportionately longer than normal, who had talked for an hour hunched in a gangly heap surrounded by discarded Kleenex and had given the impression that she would straighten up into a tall woman. But no, no more than five-five, thought Elka Willems, maybe five-six. Maybe the tall walls of the well-set Broomhill terrace had the effect of elongating her rather than diminishing her, just as well-built people appear small when inside the modern dolls' houses that for some reason, inexplicable to Elka Willems, always find eager buyers.

'I'm on day shift again, I'll try to give you progress reports every twenty-four hours.'

The women shook hands. For an instant it wasn't member of the public and police officer; for an instant, brief, profound and pregnant, it was woman on woman.

They were still there. He left home by the back door, he returned home by the back door.

Each time he entered the house they were there, each time he left they were there, leaning where he had leaned them the previous November upon his return from the Do-it-Yourself store. She never complained, never even mentioned them. He had bought them for her, carried them home, over a mile because he couldn't fit them into his small car, and left them in the kitchen, leaning against the wall. He had mumbled something about sorting them tomorrow and Rosemary, her hair in a bun, wearing blouse and skirt of pastel shades, had smiled warmly as he had peeled off his coat, hung it in the cupboard under the stairs and had knelt on the floor with Iain and they had built a tower with brightly coloured plastic bricks. Still the lengths of wood for Rosemary's kitchen shelves stood where he had propped them, and still Rosemary had not got the much requested shelves in her kitchen, and still she never complained. That afternoon, after a hurried but deeply nutritious lunch, he had put on his light summer jacket, kissed her goodbye and had walked out of the back door, past the lengths of wood, down the back garden path and as he did so she had called out, 'Take care, Richard.'

And on the journey to work the image of the wood stayed with him, and guilt gnawed at him. It struck him as odd that it seemed the longer he delayed starting on Rosemary's shelves, the harder it was to start. There was a word for that: 'inertia', he thought the word for it was 'inertia'. He drove into the car park of P Division police station and

entered by the 'staff only' door and signed in. He checked
the pigeonhole marked DC King and plucked out two
departmental circulars, the first requesting that both sides
of one piece of paper be used rather than one side only of
two sheets, and the second requesting that if possible 'phone
calls be made after 13.00 hours or at weekends when British
Telecom charges were at the standard rate. He went up to
the CID corridor and tapped on the door of Ray Sussock's
office. No answer. King pushed the door open; Sussock's
office was empty. He walked down the corridor to the room
he shared with Montgomery and Abernethy. He saw a pile
of case files on his desk, on top of which was a hastily
scribbled note:

> *Richard,*
>   *Can't hand over. Out on a 21. Everything self-explanatory.*
> *Attention drawn to Tim Moore file.*
>
>   *Ray Sussock*

King laid the note on one side and walked to the corner of
the office, hung his jacket on a peg on the hatstand and
made a cup of instant coffee. He returned to his desk and
picked up the file on Tim Moore which Ray Sussock had
left on the top of the pile, and put it on the right of his
desktop. He read the rest of the day shift's work, 'digesting
the dross' as he called it, and then picked up the Moore
file. There was little to read. He read what there was and
said, 'Blimey.' He saw what Sussock meant. Tim Moore
was not the sort of boy to go walkabout or to be with one
of a multitude of relatives all of whom might live within the
same square mile of the city. He closed the file, walked over
to a map of the city of Glasgow which was pinned to the
wall by the door. It was a newly printed map in easy to
read, eye-catching colour, greens and yellows and greys.
He located the street on which the Moore household stood.

He was not familiar with that part of the city, Rowallan Gardens in Broomhill, though he knew of it, a small quiet enclave, a few tree-lined streets which had a 'village feel' about them, despite being in easy walking distance of the city centre. He had rarely had occasion to go there: if people in Broomhill are known to the police at all they are known in their capacity of victims of crime, usually burglaries, or as Justices of the Peace, to be reverentially disturbed in the middle of the night with the request that urgently needed warrants be signed.

Looking at the map, he noted a small park at the end of Rowallan Gardens. He dismissed it. It would be the first place that a frantic parent would look. Furthermore, it would be well supervised by park keepers and populated by children and parents. Tim Moore wouldn't be there. Down the hill from Broomhill were Partick and Whiteinch, both tougher neighbourhoods than the genteel tranquillity of Broomhill, but safe as houses for children, any child in distress would not want for assistance. Victoria Park? He pondered Victoria Park and then dismissed it; again, it was well policed and well populated. His eye moved back to the Broomhill area. He noticed a bowling club with spacious grounds and beyond that an area of allotments. He considered that they too would be well supervised and probably well fenced off.

He saw the track of a disused railway line running underneath Clarence Drive, overgrown, complete with tunnel. He saw the grounds of the psychiatric hospital. Beyond that he saw the waste ground adjacent to the 'Butney' in Maryhill, so called because in the old days convicts were loaded on to lighters there, and taken down the canal to the river from where transports took them to Botany Bay.

King glanced at his watch: 14.30. There was still a lot of daylight left. Far, far better to do something than nothing. He returned to his desk and picked up the 'phone and dialled 9 for an outside line; and then, after a solid 'click' on the line, a seven-figure number.

'Strathclyde Police, dog branch.' The voice was crisp, clipped, business-like.

'DC King, P Division.'

'Yes, sir.'

'We have a missing child, a boy, ten years old. I'd like to arrange a search with the dogs of three areas near his home, please.'

'We can't provide men for a full sweep, we have committed most of our resources to a murder inquiry.'

'I see,' King replied. 'It's really just to eliminate these areas. There are three areas near his home where I think he may be likely to be if some misfortune has befallen him, if he's lying injured or is a victim of foul play. If he hasn't turned up by tomorrow we'll have to go over the areas with a tooth comb, all likely areas in fact, but for this afternoon we'll just see if he's in one of the open areas I think he may be in.'

'If he's there the dogs will find him.'

'Good. Can you attend immediately?'

'Yes, sir, we're training at the moment. I can offer six dogs with handlers. Not a lot but it's all that's available at the present.'

'Excellent. Do you need an item of clothing for his scent?'

'It's not necessary, sir. The dogs will investigate only human scent, even from shallowly buried bodies. What areas would you like searched?'

King told him, adding that he'd put a courtesy call through to the hospital administrator to advise him about the reason for the dogs and handlers in the grounds of the hospital. He replaced the 'phone with a comforting, reassuring feeling that something was being done, something was happening; he had a sense that things were moving and that he was in control. Jobs are like that, he thought: either you are on top of them or they are on top of you.

He made himself a fresh mug of coffee, sipped it while he added his contribution to the Moore file and then re-read the 'dross' from the day shift. All for information only: no action required.

There was a tap at the door. He glanced up. Elka Willems stood on the threshold. She asked, 'Do you know where Sergeant Sussock is?'

'He's got a murder.' King smiled. 'Dare say he's up to his oxters in bags and tags and confessions and denials and distraught relatives. Coffee?'

'He would have. No, no, thanks. Have you got the Tim Moore file?'

King patted it.

Elka Willems advanced towards King's desk and picked up the file. 'I've just come from the house, I'm the "interested police officer" for the family.'

'So I noted.'

'It's not a clever one, Richard. It's not clever at all.'

'Again, so I noted, and so Ray Sussock said in his note. I've just been on to the dog branch who are going to search three likely areas near his home. Just to do something really, as much as anything.'

'Good.' Elka Willems took the file and sat at Abernethy's desk, half on and half off it, one foot firmly on the ground, the other dangling in the air. 'It'll be good to tell Mrs Moore that we are doing something.'

'Any parent's nightmare.' King shook his head.

'I can only imagine.' Elka Willems glanced over King's recording and then swivelled off the desk and sat in Abernethy's chair. 'Mind if I add my bit in here?' she said. 'It won't take long.'

King said, 'Not at all.'

Elka Willems took a ballpoint pen from a mug on

Abernethy's desk which seemed to her to serve as a recep-
tacle for pens, rulers, pencils and bulldog clips on the rim.
She tried two ballpoints before she found one that worked.
'Any idea how long Sergeant Sussock is going to be?' King
thought the note of disinterest in her voice was a little
overdone, she was trawling for important personal information but trying to sound as though she was making idle
conversation.

'Your guess is as good as mine,' King replied, with an
equal note of disinterest. He wondered, as so often he had
wondered before, why she and Sussock bothered to conceal
their involvement; especially from colleagues who were
trained to observe, deduce, deduct. It seemed to him to be
a futile exercise, it seemed to him that they would be happier and more relaxed if it was out in the open. But they
played the game the way they wanted to play it.

It nagged him. Sussock leaned against the dried wooden
fencepost, his back to the field where, behind an orange
screen, Dr Reynolds would be kneeling over the curled-up
corpse of a young woman, barely twenty years old, murdered apparently by strangulation. Dr Reynolds would be
taking soil samples and insect life from around the body to
assist him in the attempt to determine how long she had
lain there in the stony Lanarkshire soil. But Sussock knew
she had not lain there long: she was too fresh.

It nagged him.

The rabbit.

The rabbit nagged him.

The little blue rabbit. A child's toy.

Of all the things in this scene of morbidity and murder
and life cut short on the threshold of adulthood, it was a
rabbit, a damn silly child's toy that preoccupied his mind,
occupying the foremost position of his mind to the exclusion
of all else.

A child had come this way recently while out on a summer's afternoon picnic with her family, had lost it, and now wept for it, or perhaps had been bought a replacement by way of compensation. It was nothing more sinister than that.

No, no, it was very sinister. Very significantly sinister. Sussock jolted himself away from the past with a stiffening of his legs and a kick with his lumbar region and stepped over the uneven grass to where McWilliams stood. The sun was high, it was he guessed about 2.30 p.m., going on 3.00 p.m. The day would start to cool from this point.

'Where's your house, sir?' Sussock stopped ten feet from McWilliams. He knew that country people like a large amount of personal space.

'Why?'

'Where is it?'

'Follow the track.' McWilliams nodded in the direction of the farm, ribbons of white cut deep into the parched green. The track led up to a wood and then seemed to turn right. A large earth-mover had been abandoned and was sitting derelict at the corner where the road turned to the right. 'Why?'

'Because I'll need to talk with your wife.'

'I'll take you up.' McWilliams turned and opened the door of the Land-Rover.

'No need,' said Sussock, 'I'll walk.'

'I don't like people talking to my wife when I'm not there.'

'I'm not people,' said Sussock coldly, 'I'm the police.'

'I still don't like it.'

'So go talk with the chaplain.' Sussock turned and began to walk up the track. He heard the door of the Land-Rover being slammed shut behind him. He peeled off his jacket and began to enjoy the stroll up the track to the Mc-Williams's house.

He was there it seemed, both eventually and suddenly, after a stroll which, while not in itself unenjoyable, he despaired would ever end, the track being a full three-quarters of a mile in length, winding between raised fields and copses. He turned yet another corner and saw a roof, and then another roof, four in all, three corrugated roofs forming a letter 'E' with the middle stroke missing, and the fourth roof of tile set back and parallel with the vertical stroke of the 'E' so that the buildings formed a square with a narrow entrance at the top and bottom corners. Sussock stopped at the corner, at a point where the track assumed a steep decline. The farmhouse and outbuildings were not just set back three-quarters of a mile from the road, but they occupied a natural hollow in the landscape concealing them from view unless one was standing above them. The nearest neighbour was probably two miles distant.

Sussock walked down the decline and entered the square formed by the house and corrugated roofed buildings. It was a square of hard concrete, swept meticulously clean, and as such seeming out of place with the overall image of the struggling tenant farmer, his searing whisky breath and ancient Land-Rover.

And no dogs. A farm with no dogs. That too surprised Sussock. It was peaceful in the courtyard, a canopy of trees beyond the buildings, blue sky, and no sound, no sound at all.

He stepped across the square and knocked on the door of the house. A sharp, respectful, yet authoritative knock.

He waited.

Silence.

A bird sang, a blackbird he guessed, richly musical. The sun beat down, the square baked. Cows lowed in the distance. He was about to knock again when the door opened with a click which seemed to Sussock to have a distinctly apologetic quality.

A frightened-looking waif stood on the threshold and blinked questioningly, submissively, at Sussock, granting the initiative and the situation immediately and unquestioningly to the stranger who had called unannounced. Sussock saw a frail woman, younger, he guessed, than she appeared to be, with darkness about her eyes which might have been mascara and a redness about her cheeks which might be blusher. But he didn't think so. He saw a frightened, hunted look in her eyes, he saw arms and legs covered, yet she occupied a hot airless house on a hot summer's day.

The woman looked at the man who had called at her house, her home, three-quarters of a mile from the lane, which was off a road, which in turn was off the main road out of Carluke, which in turn was a town whose existence was known only by its residents. She saw a tall man, a gaunt, lean face, craggy with a life which seemed to her to have been beyond fair wear and tear. She saw a weariness in his eyes, yet those eyes had an essential warmth about them. She saw the threadbare clothing of a man who cares little for himself, of a man who lives alone. She felt an affinity with the man, as if meeting a fellow traveller. She had seen before that those who have been tortured can always recognize each other, nor can they ever hide from each other.

The man spoke. He said, 'DS Sussock.' He showed her an ID card. 'I'd like to ask you some questions, if I may?'

The woman glanced over his shoulder nervously and hung on to the door at shoulder height with two sparrow-thin hands. 'My man . . .'

'He's at the end of the lane.'

'He'll tell you everything.'

'We've already spoken to him.'

'You from the city?'

'Aye.'

'What's it like there now? You've been in Garthamlock?'

'Aye.'

'Recently?'

'Aye.'

'Oh . . .' Said with a deep-felt tone, a sigh, a moan of a deeply seated need.

'Why?'

'That's where I come from. Do you know Tattershall Road?'

'Aye.' Sussock nodded. 'I know it well enough.' And he knew it fine well: low-rise, pebbled-dashed tenements, boarded-up houses, burnt-out cars, dogs in packs, litter-strewn streets, untidy gardens. The sort of scheme which comes alive only after dark. All that damp, and all that graffiti. Exist as well as you can until Thursday, that's when the Giro comes, then you get smashed, then pick out a day-to-day existence again. Aye, he knew Garthamlock fine well.

'What's it like now?' she asked again, urgently.

'Same as ever.'

'I haven't been back for twelve years. My ma and my sister stay there.'

'You don't visit?'

'No . . . my man . . .' Her voice trailed away.

'We are undertaking an inquiry,' said Sussock. 'We have found a body, a murder victim.'

'Oh . . .'

'She was buried in the field, just by the end of the lane. Maybe last night, perhaps the night before last.'

'Oh.'

'I wonder if you saw or heard anything?'

The woman shook her head. 'I don't leave the farm much. I mean the house, once a week perhaps I go to Carluke for the messages.'

'Don't or can't,' said Sussock, and he saw the woman's eyes narrow as a shaft of pain shot across them.

'We don't have a lot of money.'

It was a lame excuse. He knew it and she knew he knew it. She didn't care that he knew it, she had a sense that she and this tall man had been in similar places in life.

'Any children?'

She shook her head. 'No, I'm not bothered in a way, not here. Ordinarily . . .'

Sussock struggled to age her. Younger than her husband, significantly so, maybe ten to fifteen years. And she was frightened of something. Not just now, at this time and this place, nothing of relevance to the inquiry, but a fear which was constant and well established in her life, a fear which had worked its way to the core of her being. The darting alertness of her eyes told him so.

'So you wouldn't have heard or seen anything?'

'No. You can see for yourself. Nobody can see this place from the road, and we can't see anybody on the road. My man likes it that way.'

'Do you?'

The woman shrugged her shoulders as if to say, 'What do you think, but what can I do about it?' Then she said, 'No, my man comes in at night and he shuts the door on the world. He doesn't like people. He just wants his meals and his drink. He farms because it's the only thing he can do.'

'And you?' Sussock prodded, "Do you like people?"

The woman nodded. By now Sussock had the impression that he was speaking to a frightened child and he wondered when she had last seen a strange face. He noted no other vehicle in the yard, and wondered if she had use of the Land-Rover once a week to drive to Carluke for the messages. Or did he drive her there and back for the week's groceries. 'But you saw or heard nothing strange in the last two nights?'

'Like I said.'

Sussock stepped back, half turned, said, 'Thanks,' and

then turned back. He looked into her eyes and held them for a few seconds. 'There are places to go,' he said. 'All you have to do is get yourself to the nearest police station.'

The woman nodded gently. 'There's one in Carluke,' she said. 'I think I know where it is.'

Sussock nodded and turned away. He walked out of the yard and up the incline under the trees, following the path as it drove between fields and woods. She has been there for twelve years, she goes to Carluke weekly, and she *thinks* she knows where the police station is.

At the end of the track McWilliams waited, still leaning on his Land-Rover. Sussock approached him.

'What did she say to you?' McWilliams asked.

'Not a lot.' Sussock didn't look at McWilliams. 'She didn't see anything.'

'I told you that.' He spat into the grass.

She looked at the album. She sat on the hard worndown sofa, the sofa on which her parents had sat as long ago as she could recall, so long ago that she had once looked up at it wondering if she could climb on to it. Now she sat on it, wearing a long black dress she had bought in a cast-off shop. She sat with the curtains half drawn against the sun, ensuring a dim room despite bright daylight.

The album. She moved her head from side to side scanning the open book, compensating for the temporary loss of sight in one eye. She had fabricated a rough patch, it worked, a single eye meant single vision. The album was a collection of photographs of her guests, the guests she had had over the years, all photographed with a Polaroid, couldn't take photographs like these and send them to be developed, oh no, they'd come and take her away again and then where'd she be? But Polaroids, yes, made just for her, and people like her who want to keep little secrets safe.

This one and this one. All naked, with hands and feet

tied. All her guests down the years. It was the look in their eyes that fascinated her, that thrilled her. She traced the change in the look in the eyes of each guest as the days unfolded, the wide-eyed terror of the first two or three photographs, the slow softening of the look, so that in the last photographs taken towards the end of four or five food-less and sleepless days the eyes showed only resignation and helplessness. Then it was time for the band around the neck to end the misery and the stick to wind it with. Or the bath. Some she put in the bath. Or both, like the last one.

She had had children once. Two, all her own. Her very own.

One day they were there and the next they were gone. When she returned home they were gone. In the hospital they said, 'Do you remember anything about it, Sara? Sara, do you remember? Do you remember your children, Sara?'

'No, Doctor.' Clutching the furry toy she found in the box under the window and which she claimed as her own. 'No, I don't remember . . .'

'All right. Nurse will take you back to the ward now . . . Nurse! If you remember, Sara, if you do remember, tell nurse and I'll talk to you again.'

'Yes, Doctor.' Clutching the toy.

They walked back to the ward. Softly padding down brown corridors, locking and unlocking doors. White coats.

The kindly-eyed, black-bearded old fool. Of course she remembered, of course she recalled clearly, like yesterday, first one, then the other. 'No, no, Mummy, please.' A day between each, leaving the corpse of the first to keep the second company. 'No, Mummy, please.'

But she missed them, so she took guests. Now she had another child. A boy. She'd have preferred a girl but a boy would do. Next time it would be a girl.

He'd be getting hungry.

Tomorrow she'd photograph him. Then she'd take his clothes away.

The less food they got the more cooperative they became. She had noticed that. Some even allowed their hands to be untied and tied again and would pose for the photographs, but they were women, the girls she brought from the street with the promise of easy money, girls who had been conditioned to please. Especially if they were hungry, or were shaking because they couldn't puncture themselves.

She'd keep him for a week.

Perhaps less.

CHAPTER 3

Thursday, 18.00–23.00 hours

She was somebody's daughter. Somewhere a mother was fretting, continually going up to her daughter's bedroom to see if she had returned, to see if she had slipped home quietly and gone straight upstairs to avoid the where-were-you-last-night rumpus; somewhere a father was walking the streets because he couldn't sit still at home, he was exhausted, he would have been walking all day, still he kept going because his daughter might be round the next corner. But she wasn't in her room, and she wasn't round the next corner. She was lying on a stainless steel table, a table with a lip around the rim, a table mounted on a single central column, a hollow column so designed to allow the blood to drain away. She was on the table in a room in which stood a man dressed in a white smock. He had black, slicked-down hair and a gleam in his eye as he looked at the girl, washing her body with alcohol, doing his job diligently, thoroughly. The floor of the room was covered with industrial grade linoleum, carbolic clean. One wall of the room was given over to a huge sheet of glass, beyond which was a bank of seats, all at that moment empty. At the foot of the table on which the girl lay was a tray of stainless steel surgical instruments. The room was the post-mortem theatre in the basement of Glasgow Royal Infirmary.

A second man stood in the room. He stood reverentially, dutifully, in the corner and watched the first man with distaste. He had met the mortician before, many times before, a man who loved his work, it seemed to the second man, in the most unhealthy way. The second man was Ray Sussock. He glanced at his watch just as the digital display went from 17.59 to 18.00 which was accompanied by an audible 'peep' sound. Four hours of overtime and still no end in sight. But that was nothing new, nothing unusual in that, not for a cop in this city.

The door of the pathology lab opened. Both men looked sideways at the sudden click of the opening door. Dr Reynolds entered the room, a tall figure, his striking head of silver hair somewhat softening the effect, Sussock thought, of the white coat he was wearing. He held a small tape-recorder in his hands as he clipped the microphone to the lapel of his coat. He switched the machine on and slid it into the pocket of his coat. He walked towards the body which lay on the stainless steel table and smiled to both men as he did so. Sussock responded with a nod and a smile. The mortuary attendant said, 'Just about finished, sir.' He then withdrew to a respectful distance.

'Thank you,' said Reynolds. 'The time is 18.02 on the seventeenth of July. The deceased is a Caucasian female—' Reynolds paused and glanced up at Sussock; Sussock shook his head—'whose identity is still to be ascertained.' Reynolds attempted to move the legs of the deceased. 'I find rigor to be established, but no evidence of the onset of decomposition. Death occurred within the last forty-eight hours. There are ligature marks around the neck and bruises similar to those caused by rope around the wrists and ankles.' Reynolds paused. Sussock watched as the pathologist paid close attention to her wrists, which because of the rigor were still behind her back and so necessitated him turning the corpse half on its side. He let the body lie flat and examined the bruises on her neck. He looked up at Sussock. 'The bruises on her wrists and neck are of different ages,' he said.

Sussock was unsure whether he was being addressed, or whether the pathologist was dictating to the tape-recorder. He said, 'I see,' anyway, softly, and in passing wondered what dreadful odour might be being smothered by the heavy scent of industrial grade disinfectant which hung in the laboratory.

'And the bruising to the neck is lighter than it would be if it were the cause of death. I do not like this, Mr Sussock. All is not what it may first appear to be.'

'No, sir?'

'No, sir. The eyes are closed, not open and bulging as one would expect if she had been strangled, and as I said, the bruising around the neck is lighter than would be the case if strangulation had been the cause of death. Turning to the bruising on the ankles and wrists, I find they are anything up to a week old. The bruising about the neck is later, a few days old, two days at the most, and probably occurred at the time of death.'

'She was kept trussed up for a week before being murdered?' Sussock stepped closer to the table.

'That's not for me to say but it would certainly appear that way. It appears that she was restrained with rope for about one week, and then she died, the cause of death, however, I have still to ascertain. But it was not strangulation, despite the ligature; and despite the fact that the ligature was tightened and compressed her throat, it did not kill her.' Reynolds tapped the tips of his long fingers on the lip of the dissecting table. 'So what did?' he said to himself. 'So what did?'

'She drowned,' Richard King repeated as he compressed the 'phone between his left shoulder and ear while he held his notepad with his left hand and scribbled notes with his right. He glanced up at the digital clock on the wall and wrote 21.30 and circled the time before continuing to note the flood of information from Dr Reynolds. 'She drowned and was tied up and buried in a field.' Reynolds continued: 'I had a notion about this one. I knew it was going to be a long job, which is why I advised Mr Sussock that I could see no earthly reason for him to remain in the hospital. I did not, however, think it would take this amount of time. But I got there in the end.'

'Which is that she drowned.'

'That's the nuts and bolts of it.' Reynolds spoke calmly and unhurriedly. King knew Dr Reynolds and found the pathologist to be always calm, unhurried, meticulous and diligent: utterly professional. 'I've got an array of papers here,' he said. 'I've roughed out some notes prior to writing my report which I'll do tomorrow and have it faxed to you, once it has been typed. I hope you don't mind waiting but it's been a long day for me. Even if I did write it now there's no one to type it, not until nine in the morning, or maybe not until after that, it takes my new typist about an hour to flush the previous night's vodka from her system with black coffee. She has a problem which she has yet to confront. I digress. I can let you have the details now verbally, so you won't be held up any.'

'Of course, sir.'

'Well, it's a puzzle,' Reynolds began and, listening, King had a sense of the man settling back in his chair, 'and I confess I think that I've posed as many questions as I have answered. I'll sleep on it, but I can't come up with a solution at the moment. I've become too fogged; information overload I think you call it.'

'I know the feeling,' King said, smiling. From years of telephone work he knew that a smile can be heard.

'Right, then, details of findings.'

King flipped over a fresh sheet and held his ballpoint poised.

'There was no loosening of hair, no swelling or bloating, no desquamation of the skin . . .'

'Sorry, sir?'

'Peeling. No peeling of the skin.'

'Thank you.'

'So from that I can safely report that she was not immersed for any length of time. No more than an hour. Probably much less.'

'Right, sir.'

'So the next step was to determine whether she died by "wet" drowning or "dry" drowning.'

'I didn't know there was a difference.'

'Simply put, in "dry" drowning the drowning fluid does not penetrate the lower respiratory tract. Death, in fact, is not due to drowning at all so it is a bit of a misnomer, death actually is caused by a cardiac arrest as the fluid penetrates the nostrils and airways, which leads to a panic attack in the victim. We usually associate this type of death with the presence of alcohol or sedative drugs. The young man on a package holiday in the Mediterranean who sinks ten pints of lager at the beach bar and then decides to swim out to the diving platform is often a victim of "dry" drowning.'

'I see.'

'"Wet" drowning, on the other hand, is what might be thought of as the conventional or normal sort of drowning. Here there is actual aspiration of the drowning fluid, it's drawn not only into the lungs but into the stomach and intestines as well. It was when I opened up the deceased to find out what she had had for her last meal and found not food traces but large traces of water still present in her stomach and intestines that I was put on the right track.'

'Really?'

'Yes, really. There are, just to be complicated because nothing is ever so simple, there are two further types of drowning and the mechanisms are quite different; they are salt water drowning and fresh water drowning. The different water has different effects on the body. In fresh water drowning the body chemistry is upset, there is a rise in the level of potassium and the levels of sodium chloride, calcium, and proteins are all reduced.'

King was lost. He stopped writing but listened, dutifully.

'Drowning in salt water causes a rapid diffusion of salts into the blood vascular system and to compensate for this the body moves body fluids into the heart cavity. There is massive hypertension just before death.'

Night was falling. The office lights were on. King could make out his reflection in the window.

'The deceased,' Reynolds continued, 'died of primary rather than secondary drowning.'

'I know the difference,' said King, anxious to contribute, 'let me see if I'm right. Primary drowning is death before resuscitation, or with no resuscitation possible. Secondary drowning is those instances where the victim has been resuscitated but dies subsequently because of an infection or pneumonia or some such, which was brought on directly as a result of the immersion.'

'Yes. Good man. She was not resuscitated. There was a hæmorrhage into the middle ear which, along with the fluid in the stomach and the lower respiratory system, meant she was alive and breathing when she was immersed.'

'She went in alive and came out dead.'

'Exactly.'

'It's not an attempt to cover up murder by another means?'

'It doesn't appear to be. It appears that the ligature around the neck might have been done to cover up the drowning.'

'But why conceal the body?'

'That's one of the points I had in my mind when I said that I thought I had posed as many questions as I have answered, and pleasingly, Mr King, pleasingly, that's your job to find out. Now the fluid in the body, the drowning fluid that is, is salt water, about three per cent saline.'

'Sea-water.'

'Right. Gives you an indication of just how powerful salt is. We've all tasted sea-water, far too salty for human consumption yet only three parts in a hundred are salt. So we have a person who has been immersed in sea-water for up to an hour, about that, maybe less, who was alive when she was immersed and, as you so laconically put it, dead when she was taken out.'

'So she drowned at sea, possibly the Clyde estuary, and was driven thirty miles inland and buried in a field?'

'As I said just now about questions and answers, Mr King. And we're not out of the wood yet.'

'No?' King was both intrigued and disappointed. He enjoyed a challenge but he was beginning to feel this to be over-perplexing.

'No. You see, if a body drowns at sea, which is what we are talking about here, or so it seems, then three things happen.'

King began to scribble, for his own edification as much as anything and once more he sensed Reynolds relaxing, as if getting into his stride, as if delivering a familiar lecture to undergraduates. 'First, the body will tend to float face downwards and gravity will then pull the blood to the lowest points of the body where it will settle and congeal and cause a distinctive reddening in those areas. It's called hypostasis. So in drowning victims we find hypostasis to the anterior, the face, the front of the chest, and the lower legs and feet. In this instance it is to her back and sides. People seldom float on their backs, unless they have a life-jacket holding them that way, and they never float on their side.

'The second thing that happens is that there is often damage to the skin, everything from cuts and grazes to tears in the fingernails as the victim clings on to something for dear life, to lumps torn from the flesh where creatures of the deep have come up for a taste. Mackerel in the Clyde, for example, will leave a swimmer alone, but that swimmer has to be dead for only a few minutes—within the hour that we have mentioned—before a shoal of mackerel will attack him as voraciously as Amazon piranhas will attack a living man. In this case, there is not a blemish on the skin save for rope marks to the neck, wrists and ankles, none of which contributed to her death.

'And finally, there are the diatoms, or more appropriately in this case, there are not the diatoms.'

'Diatoms?'

'Plankton.'

'The stuff that whales eat?'

'The very same. You see, as the victim takes mouthfuls and lungfuls and then stomachfuls of sea-water, he also takes in the plankton, algæ, and plant fibres which are collectively known as diatoms. Diatoms are tough, gutsy wee beasties and work their wee way into the bone marrow, especially the marrow of the long bones. And they do this very quickly. The point is that they are not present in the bone marrow of the deceased in question.'

'Ah.' King put his ballpoint down. It rolled off his pad and on to the desktop with a hollow rattle. 'I'd like to get this right. Inspector Donoghue will be in at nine a.m. sharp. I'd like him to grasp the nuts and bolts. He can only do that if I have grasped the nuts and bolts.'

'Yes, good man, Donoghue, very good man.'

'The deceased drowned in sea-water?'

'Yes. As I said, the salinity reading of three per cent indicates sea-water.'

'But there's no corroborative evidence to support that she was actually in the sea?'

'That's a good way of putting it, Mr King. No, there is no damage to the skin, and no indication that she floated face down. She died face upwards and slightly on her side. At least, she stiffened in that position.'

'Strange,' said King.

'Very. It accords not with all previous observations of death by drowning. I'll be turning my thoughts to that over the next day or two, Mr King.' Reynolds paused. 'That's the findings in respect of the cause of death. There are one or two other things that I can tell you. She was active sexually, but there were no semen traces on the vaginal swab so she hadn't slept with anyone for a day or two prior to death.'

'The sex act was not significant in her death?'

'No. She wasn't murdered by someone who had just raped her, for example.'

King picked up his pen and scribbled.

'She had not been eating. Her stomach contained no food at all and the state of her body indicated that her body was beginning to feed on itself.'

'Starvation?'

'In a word, yes. The fat deposits had been consumed by the body. That can be replaced, but the tissue in the muscles had begun to deteriorate. The body was beginning to eat its own protein. That sort of damage can't be remedied. Starvation, as you say.'

'Could you guess as to the time lapse between last meal and exhaustion of the fat supply?'

'Four days, five.'

'About the age of the rope bruises to the wrists and ankles.'

'About that period,' Reynolds conceded. 'Now, the state of the kidneys are of interest.'

'She's a drinker?'

'No. Quite the opposite. In fact she was close to renal collapse because of fluid deprivation. Not only had she had nothing to eat for four or five days before she drowned, she had had nothing to drink either.'

'She was starving and dying of thirst?'

'Yes. Another twenty-four hours, or forty-eight at the outside, would have finished her.'

'She drowned in sea-water.'

'Yes.'

'But perhaps not at sea, as such.'

'Your department, that one.'

'And was then buried in a field.'

'That's where I met her. Again, that's a question you and your colleagues must solve. Dreadful way to end one's life.'

'Or have it ended for her.'

'Or have it ended for her.' Reynolds glanced out of his office window at the spire of the cathedral standing out against the backdrop of a calm, balmy midsummer's evening that was settling caringly, it seemed to him, and cossetingly, over Glasgow town. He decided that upon completion of the 'phone call to DC King he'd drive home, take Gustav for a walk; a walk to the hotel for a whisky, just one: a nightcap. It had been a busy day. Two cadavers. The first, a young man still in his twenties, died while walking jauntily along the pavement, his light cotton jacket slung over his shoulder. He had collapsed suddenly, no preamble, no loss of strength in his legs, one minute he was walking confident, young, healthy, the next he was prostrate with people kneeling over him anxiously or looking on with detached curiosity. A careful examination would reveal no cause for death and Reynolds had recorded a finding of 'Sudden Death Syndrome'. Such things occur from time to time. He had thought the finding was highly unsatisfactory but it was all that the present extent of medical knowledge permitted him to record. A man walks jauntily down the street, thinking of his girl, his plans, his future, pondering a chilled lager in a chrome and velvet downtown bar, and in an instant, life is snuffed out of him; death by a means which brings no warning and which leaves no trace. Until medical science took another leap forward all that Reynolds and pathologists like him could record was S.D.S. Later he had eaten tasteless salad in the hospital canteen and had then been asked to attend a locus in Lanarkshire, a young woman in a shallow grave in a field. It transpired to have been death by drowning, but not prior to starvation and fluid deprivation and apparent unlawful custody, judging by the rope marks on the ankles and wrists of the deceased.

'Or have it ended for her,' he repeated.

A pause.

In his office King sat, pencil poised over notepad.

In his office Reynolds glanced about him, he found his surroundings to be untidy in a homely sort of way. Plants, files protruding from metal drawers; a window to the east, the cathedral spire catching a glow from the dying sun to the west.

'You see—' Reynolds pulled his thoughts back on to the tracks—'from a medical point of view, from what I have been able to obtain by pure scientific observation, there is only one sign here that would point to foul play and that is the state of her kidneys.'

'Oh?'

'Yes, leaving aside the matter of the unlawful disposal of the body which is a police matter, all I can say is that the cause of death was drowning and that the drowning fluid was sea-water, we may presume the Clyde estuary, but her death by drowning could be accidental. The bruising to the neck was not fatal even though it seems to be contemporary with the time of death. The rope marks to the wrists and ankles are older than the time of death. On an elderly person or a child they might in themselves be sinister, but on a sexually active woman of her age they could have been caused by her voluntarily entering into a sex game that I personally wouldn't play, but life is life and people get their pleasures in ways strange and wondrous.' Reynolds paused and relished Richard King's restrained chuckling. 'The starvation. Again, this could be voluntary. She could have been convinced she was grotesquely overweight and had, as a result, entered into a anorexic state. You see, Mr King, there is nothing so far which points to murder, from a purely scientific point of view, until, that is, until we consider the state of her kidneys.'

'People will deprive themselves of food, but never of fluid.'

'Exactly. The human body needs fluid, but not food, not in the quantities that we in the West are given to packing away. Thirst on the other hand is, unlike hunger, increasingly painful, and associated with panic. A fear leading on to panic, a phobia, sets in if a human is deprived of fluid. I've experienced it; so, I'm sure, have you. I've downed tools in the middle of a post-mortem to get a cup of water but have happily worked on with a rumbling stomach. Thirst will prevent concentration; hunger won't. People who have been dying of thirst will be driven to drink anything, their own urine, petrol siphoned from cars, poisoned brackish water, anything, but people have to be in an advanced state of starvation before they lose discretion to that extent. Brackish water can look good after only a few hours of fluid deprivation, but it takes days of food deprivation before rotten meat or a wriggling insect looks inviting.'

'I see your point, sir.' King scribbled. 'The renal failure, near collapse, I think you said, is very significant indeed. It's the only medical observation which indicates foul play, but even so, it didn't kill her.'

'That's correct.' A walk with Gustav, a whisky. A warm bath before bed. A quiet summer's evening in the well-set south side. Reynolds began to itch to put the 'phone down just so he could pick it up again, just to tell his delectable wife, the delicious Janet, that he was sorry for having to work late but that he'd be home within half an hour or so.

'What do you think happened, sir?'

Reynolds smiled. King was like a terrier with a bone. 'I'd like to indulge you, Mr King, but I can only report the facts and perhaps comment on the likely cause of injuries.'

'I won't record it, sir. It's just for my edification and nothing else.'

'And my indulgence, Mr King.' Reynolds leaned forward, anxious now to terminate the call. 'She was, I think, held hostage for a number of days during which period she was restrained with rope. She was then drowned, probably held under water with her assailant's hands round her neck, or holding her using the rope around her neck. She was still bound at this time because otherwise her fingers would have indications that she had clawed at something. During her captivity she was given neither food nor drink. Horrific cruelty. Her captor was a man of great evil. Go and talk to a psychiatrist, he'll help you with a psychological profile of the person you're after. But that's just between you and me. Those observations won't appear in my report.'

'Understood, sir.'

'Which will be typed up tomorrow morning and faxed, as I said, before lunch. To whom shall I send it?'

'FTAO Inspector Donoghue, please, sir.'

'Yes, good man, Donoghue. He'll be back tomorrow, then?'

'Yes, sir.'

'Good.'

Reynolds replaced the receiver and picked it up again rapidly; so rapidly that he heard King replacing his receiver. He hadn't severed the line. He replaced the receiver for a second time and for a second time picked it up.

'Switchboard.' A crisp female voice.

'Outside line, please.'

'Extension, please?'

Reynolds told her and then replaced the receiver. A few seconds elapsed and then the 'phone rang. He grabbed the receiver impatiently and listened to the soft purring of the outside line. He thought it a primitive system, symptomatic of the all but dead National Health Service. It was a procedure insisted upon by the Administration largely to prevent student nurses 'phoning their great-aunts in Cornwall, and justified on the risky grounds that an emergency call would not be made *from* the hospital. Reynolds could only hope that the Administrator would continue to be proved right. He dialled his home number, he was permitted personal local calls, and told Janet that he would be home in 'about' half an hour. Having told her, he then replaced the receiver a lot more gently than he had replaced it after talking to Richard King, charming and affable and efficient as Mr King might be.

King for his part had indeed thought that Reynolds had put the 'phone down on him a little brusquely and thought that he had heard the line clicking just as he replaced his handset. But that, he thought, is the pecking order of the professions: pathologists put the 'phone down on the police, the police put the 'phone down on social workers, and social workers put the 'phone down on each other.

He sat back on his chair and glanced out of the window. The sun was setting in a burning crimson sheet somewhere over Loch Lomond. Somewhere a little boy might be dead, or he might still be alive. Somewhere a mother or father, sister or brother, did not yet know the body of their missing daughter or sister had been found and in the most sinister of circumstances. And at some point the body would have to be identified. Never, ever easy. King pulled himself forward and reached for a wad of recording sheets and began to write the nuts and bolts of Dr Reynolds's findings in a report format as reported to him on 17/7, at—he glanced at his watch—21.40 approx.

This done, he replaced the recording on the file and pondered the next move. He thought of Inspector Donoghue, a mild-mannered man, a gentleman, King had found, a man of quiet authority who held King in awe of his cold stare and raised eyebrow.

King pondered. He picked up the 'phone and dialled a two-figure internal number.

'Collator.' A crisp punctilious voice.

'DC King. Reference a missing person.'

'Very well, sir.'

'A female.' King heard the soft tapping of a computer keyboard being punched. 'Early twenties . . . could you widen that to late teens . . . Caucasian . . . brown hair, eyes blue, no apparent distinguishing features . . . probably missing for a week now . . .'

'I'll go back to the beginning of the month, sir. I'll have the files on any likely candidates sent up to you.'

'I'd appreciate it.' King replaced the 'phone, picked it up and then replaced it again. No. Sussock had told him that Bothwell couldn't dust the car for prints until the morning, he had informed him of that when he had returned to the station to sign off and hand over. The car had been identified as having been stolen from the grounds of Yorkhill Hospital one week earlier. The owner had been contacted. He wanted his car back and understandably was 'not best pleased', as Sussock said, when told he couldn't have it, not so soon, anyway.

King drummed his fingers on the desktop. He couldn't proceed with the car, even it if was linked to the murder. There was still the possibility that the car's presence at the locus was nothing other than a coincidence. He leafed through the thin but growing file on the deceased and noted that a 't' had not been crossed, or an 'i' dotted: he consulted the file and 'phoned the home of the car owner.

'He's no in,' said a woman's voice; a child cried in the background, a wailing sound. An infant teething? 'When are we going to have our car back, my man's got a terrible journey to work and back without the car, so he has.'

'As soon as we've finished with it, madam.' King spoke soothingly. 'Where is your husband?'

'At his work.'

'Which is?'

'Springburn Depot. British Rail.'

King 'phoned Springburn Depot. 'Driver Nicol? Yes, he's working at the moment. Where? Somewhere between Queen Street and Stirling. Yes, he was on duty yesterday evening.'

'No,' said King, in answer to a question which he thought was more of an invasion of privacy than anything else. 'No, there's no problem at all. Mr Nicol is under no suspicion at all. Thank you.' He replaced the 'phone and entered the call in the continuation sheet. The owner of the vehicle, Mr Nicol, was driving a locomotive between Queen Street and Stirling at the likely time of the burial of the body in a

Lanarkshire field. Even if the car was connected with the murder, its owner could be eliminated from inquiries. It was something he had contributed, small negative in a sense, but neat, he felt. An 'i' dotted, a 't' crossed.

There was a tap on the door of the CID room. King looked up. A young fresh-faced constable stood on the threshold, files in his arms. He seemed to King to be nervous, as if still finding his feet, at that stage where everything is still new. King recalled when he was like that.

'The files,' the young constable said. 'The collator asked me to bring them to you, sir.'

King smiled. He held out his hands, the young constable stepped forward and handed the files to him and withdrew, nervously. King laid the files on his desk, seven in all. He began to read them, writing the names of the missing females as he came to each file, and then finding a detail or a fact that enabled him to eliminate the possibility that this one of the missing girl was the girl whose body was taken from a shallow grave earlier that day, he scored the name off the list. One girl was Asian; another had given birth by Cæsarean section, something that Dr Reynolds would not have overlooked. Two had the wrong colour of hair. He was left with four possible victims, four girls, four young women who had been reported as missing over the last eleven days, all of whom were the same age group and similar overall appearances as the girl who lay in a steel drawer in the mortuary of the GRI. In each file was a photograph of the missing person, with the name of the missing person written on the rear of the photograph in a neat hand. King took each photograph and placed it in a brown paper envelope and sat back in his chair. The next step could take the inquiry forward most handsomely, but it was a step he found himself reluctant to take. If one of the photographs was that of the deceased, then one of the missing persons was dead, one family could give up hope and start to grieve. One family would have a knock on the door, perhaps close to midnight, be asked to accompany the police to the mortuary. Then he sat forward. 'Let's do it,' he said to himself. So loud that his voice echoed in the empty room, but none the less he said it to himself.

In the mortuary a solemn attendant, with a nursing sister looking on, withdrew a drawer and parted a sheet, exposing the full face of a young girl. It was a small face, a pert nose, slightly protruding teeth, but not at all unattractive. King studied the features and then took a photograph from the envelope. It was the first photograph, but he looked at the other three anyway. Her name was Sandra Shapiro and she would have been twenty years old in three days' time.

King nodded his thanks and the drawer slid silently and solidly shut. He walked away from the mortuary, up a long, slightly inclined rubber-matted corridor and found himself wondering about the emotions that had been felt within this solemn place, this awful walk: the trepidation and the thread of hope on the decline, the devastation and shock and partner-clinging grief on the incline. It was a long corridor and King felt that to be a most sensitive gesture, it meant the dead house was far removed from the bustle of the main building, where people were repaired and discharged, of tea-rooms and notice-boards, of visiting hours and flowers for the sick. It was wholly fitting and proper to walk a long silent walk to the house of the dead, and to walk a long silent walk back.

He emerged into the main rotunda of the GRI, went out by the swing doors and walked across the car park. It was a calm, warm night, a high cloud layer obscured the stars.

He drove back across the city through the grid system. The pubs were turning out, street Turks jostled and shouted, some in good humour, some not. A man sat up against a wall, two cops in black trousers and white shirts stood over him, one talked on his radio, a small crowd had gathered. King drove on. He drove along Bath Street and hit a sequence of green lights. More revellers, cops with a high profile, two fire-appliances, klaxons and blue lights, a taxi screeching, hanging a U-turn. Glasgow. Night.

King walked into P Division police station via the rear 'staff only' door. He went to the front of the building to the uniform bar and signed in the movements book. A man, a member of the public, stood at the uniform bar, a constable was speaking to the man. The duty officer sat at his desk struggling with a typewriter, slowly 'hunting and pecking' his way through an incident report. King checked his pigeonhole for messages. None. He went up the stairs to the CID corridor, taking them two at a time. He opened the file on the murdered girl, recorded his visit to the mortuary and entered his observation that the identity of the deceased appeared to be Sandra Shapiro, nineteen years and three hundred and sixty-two days old. He cross-referenced the murder file to the missing persons file of the same name. He stood and walked to the corner of the room and fixed himself a coffee. As he was spooning the granules into his mug he recalled with no little amusement the legendary report on a trainee police cadet at the end of a training placement: 'he made himself coffee in the sergeant's mug.' The story had obscure origins and was certainly apocryphal but was none the less guaranteed to bring hoots of derisive laughter whenever it was recounted. Mug of coffee in hand, King returned to his desk and picked up the missing persons file on Sandra Shapiro.

She had been reported as missing five days previously by her father, who had an address in Egypt. Interestingly, and probably not known by her father, Sandra Shapiro had a little track: two counts of reset and one of soliciting. This last King thought would certainly not be known to her father, not if King knew Egypt where roses grew on lattices on the walls of neat houses. The track was useful: very, very useful. It meant her fingerprints would be on file, which in turn meant that the identity of the corpse could be confirmed or otherwise. Her parents might of course view the body if they wished, but a formal, emotional, identification might not be necessary after all. King hoped so because such ordeals were never easy.

Three males drank liquid.

The first stood at the bar of the Inverleithen Hotel in Pollokshaws. He was a tall man, slender, a striking head of silver hair, a St Bernard lying patiently at his feet. He swilled the last of the whisky around his glass. He smiled to himself. About him, patrons were standing and helping each other into coats and nodding good-nights. Not here the mad stampede to the bar when the burglar alarm is switched on for a few seconds to announce last orders; here the patrons know when closing time falls, and drink up and slip away without fuss.

'Another drink before I shut the bar, sir?' The hotelier stood in front of Reynolds and slipped a starched teacloth over the beer pumps.

'No, no, thanks,' said Reynolds.

'You look happy, sir, like the cat that got the cream.'

'Do I?' Reynolds continued to smile. He drained the glass and placed it on the polished mahogany bar. He shook the dog's lead. 'Come on, Gustav, home time.' The St Bernard levered itself to its feet. 'Something occurred to me,' Reynolds explained. 'The obvious. I couldn't see it at first, came home, had dinner, took Gustav out for a stroll, had a nightcap, and standing here, I saw it as clear as daylight.'

The second man sat in a huge room. He sat on the settee and gently and tenderly held the hand of the lady who sat beside him. He looked about him, a cavernous room in a cavernous West End tenement near Atholl Gardens, just behind Byres Road, and he sipped his drink, a tall glass containing mineral water with just a hint of white wine. Eight people were at the soirée, three couples were the guests, and the hosts made up the fourth couple. They were people in the media, in the main. They were unknown and wary of each other and had throughout the evening sat around the walls and corners of the room, talking softly and in a restrained, polite manner, and afforded each other a considerable amount of personal space. The music was soft and classical and came from another room in the tenement, a room at the far end of the hallway, at the opposite end of the flat. It was, thought the man, the device of someone who, if he owned a country estate instead of a Glasgow tenement, would have a lake constructed in the furthest reaches of his land, so that the water would glisten tantalizingly in the distance when viewed from the owner's drawing-room.

The man drained his glass and looked at his watch. He turned to his partner and said, 'Duty calls,' and then to his host, 'I'm sorry, but I have to leave. It's been a pleasant evening. Thank you.'

'Duty calls,' echoed the host.

Malcolm Montgomerie stood, tall, chiselled features, downturned moustache. 'That's the long and the short of it,' he said. He found the host's attitude mocking and supercilious.

'Thanks for coming.' The host smiled but didn't stand. 'Going and the night's so young.'

The third male huddled in the darkness. His throat had constricted, his tongue felt too large for his mouth. He ached for water. He sat back against the wall of the room. It was cold. Very, very cold. Then he realized that it wasn't cold; it was wet.

It was wet.

The wallpaper was damp. He turned. He pressed the paper with his palm and then took his palm away. His hand was moist. He licked the moisture from his hand and pressed the wallpaper again. More moisture glistened on his hand. He licked it off and then pressed the wallpaper with both hands.

CHAPTER 4

Friday, 04.30–12.30 hours

She had reached that poignant phase in life when for the first time she saw the young in the old. She saw the young man in the old man huddled over his watered down whisky, she saw the young woman in the old lady walking down the street with her white stick and shopping trolley. It had come to her quickly, overnight it seemed, and it had happened recently. Before that, she had never been able to see the young in the old, the old woman had in her eyes always been old, but now really, for the first time, she saw Sussock as a young man.

Something that night had made her waken. No sound, no sense of ill health, but something, something akin to the way that one person can stand silently at the foot of the bed of a slumbering person and if he stands there long enough, but for a period measured only in minutes, then the sleeper will waken. And so it was that she woke, stirred, reached out a hand to rest on his thigh and, finding the bed empty, turned and shook herself into a sense of alertness. She glanced around her room, softly illuminated by the street lamp just below the window, the double bed was in a recess of a sitting-room decorated in pastel shades with a Van Gogh print on the wall. It was her home, a room and kitchen, ideal for a single young person, but it had been built at the turn of the century for a family to occupy.

Days of overcrowding, and no internal sanitation but a common toilet on the stair. Such living conditions were well within living memory. She slid silently from beneath the duvet and stood on the comfortable pile of the carpet, tall, statuesque, long of limb and slender of waist, with her blonde hair cascading over her shoulders. She walked gracefully around the foot of the bed on the balls of her feet and out of the room into the short corridor and stood on the threshold of the kitchen, with recently installed shower cubicle to her left.

The light shone from the common stair, through the opaque glass above the door, sufficiently to illuminate the kitchen. Sussock sat at the kitchen table, also naked, comfortable to be so in the warm July night. She leaned against the frame of the door and looked at Sussock and as she stood and looked she saw a troubled man. He sat still, one leg slightly more extended than the other, a slightly protruding stomach, but far thinner and in better condition than many men of his vintage. His head was bowed forward and his hands clasped his face. He became aware of her presence. He took his hands from his face and turned to her, beautiful in his eyes. And she saw him, as a young man; it was as if, when her perception changed, he had shed years.

'Ray?' She approached him with soft slow feminine movements and knelt beside him and laid a slim hand of long fingers on his leg. 'Ray. What's wrong?'

'So, I did wake you.' Sussock sat back. He looked up at the ceiling and then lowered his gaze and looked at the lights from the tenements across the back courts. Elka Willems recognized the reaction. She had seen it so many times before, the grief reaction of the newly bereaved, the taking on board of an enormity so huge that one had no room for it in one's life, yet one must find room because it is reality, the realization that struggling against it is futile.

She squeezed his leg and he let his hand fall gently on her wrist. And she had seen this too; the need for human contact at such times is all-consuming. She had, often, ached for the suddenly widowed who had had to go home for the first time to a cold and empty house. She didn't press him. He was squeezing her hand, he knew she was there, he'd tell her in his own time.

'I woke up, shouting,' he said. 'I was pleased I hadn't disturbed you, but I had. I've only just come through.'

A pause. The sound of a motorbike driving along the road, behind the tenements whose lights shone over the back courts.

'There's another one,' he said softly.

'Another one?'

'This afternoon, yesterday afternoon, I was late getting off, the murder.'

'The body in the field?'

'I've been there before.'

A silence. He'd explain.

'There was a child's toy in a pathway next to the field, a furry toy, a rabbit, a blue rabbit, it's been bagged and tagged, we have it safe in productions . . .' He was beginning to ramble and stopped himself. He breathed deeply. 'I've seen it before.'

'A furry toy?'

'At the same place, more or less, within a half mile I'd say, if I remember.'

'So, a furry toy is found in a lane. A child has dropped it.'

'A furry toy close to where we found an abandoned car which had been stolen, neatly parked and locked.'

'Oh . . .'

He squeezed her hand. 'That was twenty-five years ago.'

A silence. A resonance.

'There's a body out there, Elka, I know. You can call it

what you like, the intuition of an old and jaded cop, but there's a body in those fields and its been there for twenty-five years.'

'Oh, Ray . . .'

'I was a constable, considered experienced but still a constable, and I attended just like Hamilton and Piper attended this afternoon. We contacted the owner and he came out in his mate's car and drove his own away, no damage to it, and nobody came by to point out a freshly dug grave in the field a few yards away and in fairness, I don't recall seeing anything amiss, but I'm not a country man, signs like that would be lost on me. I can read a street but I'd trip over something out of the ordinary in the country and I'd still not notice it. But I remember clearly walking up and down near the car, waiting for the owner to arrive, it was just about this time of year, too, and I remember seeing a furry toy. It sticks in my mind because it was lifelike and lifesize, and in my naïvety . . . seems so stupid, but I thought: What a brilliantly coloured rabbit and see how it's standing still to avoid detection, playing possum. And that's the reason I remember, not because of seeing it but because of the sense of embarrassment and also the relief that I had been alone when I realized that I'd been creeping up on a toy.' He shook his head. 'I wanted to see how close I could get before it bolted. I remember the incident clearly. Emotions, you don't forget them as easily as sights. That's why I woke, something was troubling me all evening, and that's what it is, I'm sorry about earlier . . . I thought I was just tired.'

''S all right.' She patted his thigh. 'It doesn't have to be perfect every time.' She kissed his leg. 'With you it's beautiful most of the time and that's good enough for this lady.' He rested his hand on her head and let it run down her silk-like hair to the nape of her neck and then below to her muscular back and began to run his hand over her shoulder-blades in wide circular movements.

'But that's it, that's what it was. That's what was troubling me. I woke up, shot bolt upright, shouting. I couldn't take it all in. I wanted to thrash my arms and legs about, you know the way. I didn't want to wake you up and so I came in here. I wanted to bang on the tables and the walls.'

'Well, I'm awake now.'

He brought his fist down hard on the table. Twice. 'Thanks,' he said.

'I know the feeling, but no more. I've got neighbours and we make enough noise as it is. I see the way they smile at me in the mornings.'

'I'll have to tell Fabian. I'll have to tell him first thing.'

'It's your day off tomorrow.'

'I could 'phone, but I'll go in. Frankly, I'd rather go in than do what I intended to do, which was go to Shrew and collect my new summer raincoat and a few other odds and ends. I've been putting off doing it for a while. I'll do both in the morning and then have the afternoon and evening free: we still have a dinner date, and I wouldn't enjoy the meal if I hadn't first disclosed to Fabian about the possibility of a second body being out there.'

'Of course. I suppose that means the car is linked to the body?'

'Sorry?'

'You said that there was no direct link between the stolen motor and the body, but now you've recalled a similar incident twenty-five years ago, same place, a toy rabbit . . .'

'Of course,' he said again, as he continued to stroke her back. 'We'll still need more than that, but yes, you're right, there now is a link between the car and the body. What a way to spoil a night's sleep. But at least I can wake up.'

Elka Willems stood and he sensed her body scent. She laid a hand on his shoulder.

'You know,' he said taking her hand in his, 'that's my greatest complaint about police work, that it deprives you of the luxury of self-pity.'

'Come to bed, Ray,' she said softly. 'Come back to bed: now.'

Fabian Donoghue drove his Rover into the car park at the rear of P Division police station. An observer, a pedestrian perhaps, would have noted a fluid, controlled, masterful handling of the controls. The journey from his bungalow in Edinburgh, his wife and two children, had taken just over an hour; not an impossible commuting time. He parked his car in his allotted parking space close to the 'staff only' door and pulled his gold hunter from the pocket of his waistcoat. It was 08.29. He slipped the watch back into the pocket and let the chain hang in a modest loop. He locked his car and walked towards the building. He enjoyed the air that morning, fine and sunny, even in the centre of the city the air still had a freshness about it. There was a spring in his step. He held his head high. He was ready for the world.

He signed in, plucked two circulars from his pigeonhole and went upstairs to the CID corridor. He stopped at the doorway of the room occupied by the detective-constables. Malcolm Montgomerie sat back in his chair, eyes closed, feet on his desk. A pile of files stood on the edge of the desk.

''Morning, Montgomerie.'

Montgomerie sat bolt upright and slammed his feet on to the floor, as if jolted by a surge of electricity. ''Morning, sir.'

'About five minutes, Montgomerie,' Donoghue said coldly. 'Give you time to wake up.'

Donoghue went to his office, put his hat on the peg of the coat-stand and sat in his chair. He tore yesterday's date from the calendar and read the legend that day: *Those who give, get.*

'Quite true,' he said to himself.

Settling in his chair, he took his pipe from his pocket, a briar with gently curving stem, and from his other pocket he took his tobacco pouch and began to knead the tobacco into the pipe bowl. His was a special mix; made up for him by a tobacconist in George Square, it had a Dutch base with a twist of dark shag to produce a deeper flavour and to slow the burning rate. He closed his tobacco pouch and laid it on his desk to the side of the ashtray; large enough, it had been quipped, to swim a couple of fish in. He held his pipe in one hand while 'teasing' the tobacco with the fingertips of the other. Putting the stem in his mouth, he took his gold-plated lighter and placed the flame over the bowl, sucking and blowing as he did so. It was, as usual, his first pipe of the day and was, as usual, by far the most enjoyable. He glanced out of the window as he slid the lighter back into his jacket pocket, saw the sun glinting off the square, angular steel and concrete buildings at the bottom end of Sauchiehall Street, on the pavement thronged with people, the street itself full of buses, of varying livery courtesy of the recent de-regulation of the bus services. His particular favourite was the striking yellow on blue of the Kelvin Scottish bus company whose vehicles always seemed to be gleamingly clean.

There was a reverent tap at his door. Donoghue turned and said, 'Come in, Montgomerie. Take a pew.'

Montgomerie entered Donoghue's office carrying an armful of files and sat in the chair in front of Donoghue's desk. Donoghue sat in his chair and noticed that Montgomerie appeared to have washed his face, there was still a little moisture on his brow and he detected the unmistakable aroma of liquid soap. Whiskers were beginning to appear on Montgomerie's chin.

'Quiet night?'

'Very quiet, sir.' Montgomerie laid the files on the floor.

'There are two major inquiries to hand over, sir, both started on yesterday's back shift.'

'No action in the wee small hours, then?'

'Not on the two major cases, sir.'

'Right, we'll keep them to the end. Let's shift the dross first, shall we, weed the garden before we dig it.'

'Very good, sir.' Montgomerie reached down beside him and picked up the first case.

The 'dross' or the 'garden weeds' Donoghue found to consist of a spate of car thefts, two burglaries, one particularly messy involving the near-destruction of the interior of the property; a mugging in the city centre. 'A bit embarrassing,' said Montgomerie, 'victim was a foreigner, came to experience the legendary warmth of the city of Glasgow.'

'Not been too busy then, Montgomerie.'

'Quiet, as I said. I've really just been taking witness statements and visiting the locuses. They really made a mess of that house, sir, ugh, horrible. The owners have moved into a hotel. I can't say I blame them.'

'What happened to the foreigner, the tourist?'

'The Youth Hostel put him up, sir. A young man in his twenties. I soft-soaped them a bit, you know, victim of a crime, visitor to the city, a guest here, and they agreed to put him up and give him some fodder. He's going to the bank today to arrange for money to be wired to him here. Best we could do.'

'Description of the attacker?'

Montgomerie shook his head. 'From behind. All over before the victim knew what was happening.'

'An experienced mugger?'

'Sounds like it, sir.'

'Mark that one for action, give it to day shift which is . . .'

'Abernethy, sir.'

A pause.

'Sergeant Sussock's day off, sir.'

'Oh, I see. Well, speak to Abernethy. Ask him to pull all known neds and felons with this sort of track. And that's it?'

'Just the two big ones, sir.'

Donoghue sat back and pulled on his pipe and listened attentively as Montgomerie recounted the two 'big ones'. As Montgomerie spoke, Donoghue inched forward, fraction by fraction, unaware of himself doing so, as details of the missing child were related, worrying enough in itself, but eclipsed by the story of the body found in a shallow grave in a field beside a red road in Lanarkshire. But none the less, Donoghue could not blame Montgomerie for ending the graveyard shift with his eyes closed and his feet on the desk. He couldn't have taken either inquiry an inch further forward.

'All right.' Donoghue took his pipe from his mouth and examined the bowl. 'All right, you hand the mugging to Abernethy and I'll speak to him about it later, we can't give this any sort of priority but it would help international relationships if we could arrest the felon, or felons, keep our end up in the eyes of Interpol. Where does our guest come from, incidentally?'

'Torquay,' Montgomerie said, smiling, 'he's an Englishman.'

'Just give it to Abernethy.'

Montgomerie left the room still smiling at his own joke, carrying all the files he had brought with him save for two which Donoghue retained. Donoghue, alone again, refilled his pipe and began to read the files, digesting the contents. Twenty minutes later he laid the files down. He didn't like either. He thought that observations contained in both files were valid. Of the Tim Moore case, it was valid to point out that boys of Tim's social milieu don't wander off and visit a relative. If they go missing, they have been abducted.

It's a fear which haunts every parent, a prospect which strikes terror into the heart of any parent. He thought that Richard King had done a good job by organizing a search of likely areas near the family home. Three areas all told. No result: that he felt was good and bad. It meant hope could be kept alive, but so was fear. And with the passing of each hour hope fades slightly and fear increases. He reached for the 'phone on his desk and dialled a two-figure internal number.

'Uniform bar,' said a crisply efficient male voice.

'DI Donoghue.'

'Yes, sir.'

'Can you locate WPC Willems and DC Abernethy, they'll be in the building somewhere. Ask them to come to my office, please. As soon as you like. Thank you.'

Tim Moore's disappearance might be sinister; in fact, Donoghue thought that it had all the hallmarks of a very sordid affair. But the body in the shallow grave in a Lanarkshire field undoubtedly was sinister. It had the certain hand of another or other players about it. He picked up the file on the person believed to be Sandra Shapiro of Egypt and, reading it, had to concede that as in the recording in Tim Moore's file, the observations were valid. There was as yet no actual evidence of murder because death had been due to drowning. So far the most serious charge that could be preferred was that of interfering with the office of the Coroner, otherwise known as unlawful disposal of the dead, which carried a maximum sentence of four years. But it was early days yet, very early days.

He pulled on his pipe.

He was amused by Dr Reynolds's confusion at the lack of diatoms in the marrow of the long bones, which ought to be present if the victim had died at sea. Donoghue thought that perhaps Dr Reynolds was a little too immersed in the post-mortem, a little too close to it. He thought that the pathologist ought to step back a little, take the dog for a walk, have a drink in a quiet bar, perhaps. It seemed obvious to Donoghue that the girl had drowned in a saline solution, in a bath for example, or had been drowned, and then immediately after death had been pulled out of the bath and laid on her side with the hypostasis forming where her body touched the floor. The real question was, how did she come to drown? Was it deliberate murder, was it as postulated by King in his recordings of his conversation with Dr Reynolds, as indicated by the rope marks, an ill-advised sex game which had gone horribly wrong? Such things do happen from time to time, but the surviving partner is often wise enough to call the police immediately and offer a full explanation. But it has also been the case that the surviving partner has panicked and has attempted to conceal the body and cover his tracks.

Donoghue glanced out of his office window, the blue sky, the sun already high: he thought that there would be many a man and woman out there who would be remarking on the pleasantness of the day. For him, reading the files, the day was beginning to cloud over, just as many a deep mid-winter's afternoon had been brightened with the concluding of a long inquiry.

There was a tap on his door: soft, reverent.

'Come in,' said Donoghue, and only then looked up. Abernethy lean and gauche, and Elka Willems, stood in the doorway. 'Come in.' Donoghue smiled. 'Come in and pull up a seat.'

The two young officers sat, Abernethy in his early twenties, new to CID work, still finding his feet but Donoghue was more than satisfied that he was getting there; Elka Willems, her blonde hair now done in a tight bun and still devastatingly attractive despite the unflattering uniform of a WPC, so much so that Donoghue was instantly reminded of the shock waves which travelled through the building when she first arrived, having transferred from Stranraer.

'The Moore case.' Donoghue patted the file.

'Yes, sir.' Elka Willems responded knowingly.

'Has Montgomerie had a word with you about the mugging last night, Abernethy?'

'Yes, sir. He has.'

'I'd like you to handle it. Give the details of the offence to the collator and ask him to provide you with names of likely suspects and take if from there. I'd also like you to work with WPC Willems on the Tim Moore case. If you don't know about it, WPC Willems here will fill you in. In fact, here's the file.' Donoghue tossed it to the edge of his desk. Abernethy reached forward and picked it up. 'I don't like the feel of this one, not at all, time for a house-to-house, I think. Visit his school, speak to the other children, one of them might have seen him getting into a car, one of them might have been approached by a stranger about the time he was abducted. There's also a good man at the University —Glasgow University—Department of Psychology, a Dr Cass; I've picked his brains before and he's proved to be a real goldmine, you could give him a bell.'

'Very good, sir.'

'You might ask him for a psychological profile of the sort of person who would be likely to abduct children and if your house-to-house throws up a likely description which might match the profile . . . We'll trace him and bring him in for a chat.'

'Or her,' said Elka Willems.

'Or her.' Donoghue nodded. This was the late twentieth-century and he had grown to fear the sting of the angered feminist.

Abernethy and Willems stood and left his office, walking silently out of the room. They turned the corner, were lost from his sight, but he looked up as he heard the mutter of pleasantries with a rising inflection of surprise, echoing in the corridor. Seconds later Ray Sussock tapped on his door. 'A word, sir,' he said.

Donoghue sat back. 'Come in, Ray, take a seat.' It was proving to be a busy start to this particular working day, first Montgomerie, then Abernethy and Elka Willems, and now, with no little surprise, Ray Sussock calling in on his day off. Donoghue looked at Sussock as he sat in the chair recently occupied by Abernethy and once again was struck by the weariness about him, the drawn haggard expression in his face, a man overdue for retirement, a man who could take his retirement now for the asking, but 'personal reasons, sir' kept him at the sharp end of police work, and kept him doing a young man's job. 'So what's on your mind that you come in on your day off, pleasant as it is to see you.'

'Do you know what you were doing twenty-five years ago, sir?'

'Still at school.' Donoghue smiled and scraped the charred tobacco from his pipe bowl into the ashtray. He split the stem of his pipe and took a pipecleaner from his desk drawer. 'Deciding whether to stay on and try for University or follow my dad into the shipyards. He was an electrician and could have got me started. Why do you ask? What were you doing twenty-five years ago?'

'I was a constable. No longer a cub, no longer wet behind the ears, considered experienced, in fact, not a sergeant though, not then, that came later.' He glanced to one side, then looked at Donoghue and held eye contact. 'I was standing guard on a recently discovered stolen car in a country lane and I decided to creep up on a rabbit . . .' He began to relate the tale but already Donoghue's scalp was crawling and his fingers fell limp around his pipe bowl and stem, as within his brain alarm bells jangled, jangled, jangled.

He allowed Sussock to relate the story without interruption, held the pause when Sussock had finished and eventually said, 'Good Lord, Ray. A stolen car, neatly parked, a rural location, a child's toy rabbit, identical to the locus of yesterday's grim discovery, except that twenty-five years separates them. It means, I think, that we have to assume that the car we found yesterday is implicated in some way after all. Most probably it was stolen to transport the body in.'

'That's what I thought too, sir.'

'It's all too much of a coincidence.' Donoghue shook his head. 'In fact, it's not a coincidence. I think that we can't ignore the possibility that there is a body in a field close to where you stood guard all those years ago. We'll have to search for it. Can you remember the location?'

Sussock nodded wearily. His day off was disappearing fast. 'You see, the thing that worries me, sir, is that if there is a body out there, and if they are connected—that is, that they are both down to the same felon—then how many more are there, how many more were done in the period between? And of the one I was standing guard near, if it's there, is it the first one? Or were there others even before that? How many bodies are we talking about?'

Donoghue raised his eyebrows. 'Let's take one stage at a time, Ray.'

'Yes, you're right, sir.'

'I take it that you don't mind giving up your free time, Ray? I know that it's been twenty-five years and one day won't make a great deal of difference but it's the sort of thing that would nag me if I didn't address it.'

The 'phone on his desk rang.

'I feel the same way, sir. I just wouldn't enjoy my free time with this on my mind.'

'Good man. If you can recall the area where the car was found, we'll search from there, taking the distance of the grave from the car at yesterday's location as our model. We'll need a sergeant and half a dozen men.'

'I'll arrange it now, sir.' Sussock stood.

Donoghue picked up his 'phone. 'Donoghue.'

'Dr Reynolds for you, sir.'

'Reynolds here.'

''Morning, sir.'

'Mr Donoghue, good. I gather that you will by now have been apprised of the PM result of the girl who was found in the field?'

'The one who drowned?'

'That's the one. I'm a slow thinker, Mr Donoghue, or I'm probably too close to the job in hand, but I've managed to come up with a solution to the puzzle of the missing diatoms. The answer came to me over a whisky last night.'

'Oh?'

'I was puzzled why there were no diatoms, and why the hypostasis was in the wrong place for a drowning victim.'

'Yes?'

'The answer is obvious. She drowned in a bath or container which contained saline solution, which in turn was by design or accident three per cent salt, the same as seawater, and after she drowned she was pulled out and laid on the floor where the blood settled in the parts of her body which touched the floor. Simple, really.'

Donoghue smiled. 'Thank you, sir, that helps us a lot, an awful lot, narrows the inquiry. Means we're looking for an inside locus. While you are on the 'phone, can you tell me how possible it would be to identify someone who was murdered twenty-five years ago and has since that time been buried in the same manner as the girl about whom we speak?'

'Well.' Reynolds paused. 'You could sex the remains immediately, any doctor can tell at a glance whether it was a male or female skeleton, because after twenty-five years a skeleton it would be. After that, the teeth would be the most reliable source of information, they won't decompose and if you have any idea of the deceased's identity you can get her dental records, they'll be filed somewhere and are as unique as fingerprints or a DNA profile. Otherwise it's police work, identification by means of non-degradable artefacts found with the body: watches, rings, contents of a leather purse or wallet, but as we speak I remember that there is a technique for rebuilding the face and head using the skull as a base, it was pioneered by a Soviet scientist. You may have seen the film *Gorky Park*.'

'I have, yes.'

'The technique featured in that film, it has been adopted and is used in the UK, as you may know.'

'I did. I've never had occasion to use it.'

'Neither have I, it's a field of Medical Art. Why do you ask? Do you have another investigation in hand?'

'No, not yet,' said Donoghue. 'We may, just may, have another body, and if we do it will be part of the same investigation.'

'Good heavens.' Reynolds sighed. 'And a twenty-five-year gap between them.'

'That's the way it appears, sir,' said Donoghue. 'I'll certainly be in touch if we do find another corpse.'

Elliot Bothwell blinked and moved clumsily as he worked the paper round first one ink-stained finger and then the next, and then the next. It was times like this that the job got to him: in this instance the fingerprinting of a corpse in the mortuary of the GRI as a nursing sister and mortuary attendant looked solemnly on, ensuring reverence for the dead and being present as a witness in Elliot Bothwell's best interest lest a complaint of impropriety be levelled at him. But whatever he did, whatever he had to do, he knew that he would not return to his old job, not no way, not for a pension. His old job was that of chemistry assistant in a tough inner city secondary school, where in the course of his years there he had mixed the same calm chemicals in the room behind the chemistry laboratory, all the while watching the chemistry teacher's hair turn grey as the man attempted to teach intake after intake of uninterested adolescents. Then one day, while browsing through the Regional Council vacancy list, Bothwell saw the post of forensic chemist with the Strathclyde Police being advertised. He applied. He was interviewed. He was offered the post. He didn't look back. Most of the work, interesting at first, had become routine. Most crime is petty, but even then he found that no two jobs are quite the same, mostly he dusted stolen cars or scenes of burglary for felons' latents, but occasionally, just occasionally, there was a stomach-churning job to be done, as in lifting the prints of a young woman who had in life been attractive. Elliot Bothwell was thirty-six, he still lived with his mother in a three-roomed apartment in Queens Park, up a china-tiled 'wally close', of stained wood, heavy doors and brass knockers. He wouldn't go back to his old job, not now, not for a pension.

He transferred the impression of the tenth finger by firm steady pressure on to the card in the appropriate box, left index, and stood. He clamped his plastic work case shut and blinked at the nurse.

'Finished?' she asked, smiling.

Bothwell nodded. 'Uh-huh. That's it. Doesn't take long, really.'

The nurse nodded at the mortuary assistant and then she and Bothwell left the mortuary and began the long walk back to the main building, the walk walked earlier by Richard King, and earlier than that by Ray Sussock. The nurse and he didn't speak on the walk along the inclined corridor, save: 'Busy these days?'

'Yes,' said Bothwell. 'Always busy. Back to dust a car now, part of the same inquiry, I believe.'

Mrs McWilliams sat in the kitchen of her home. She rubbed her ribs, massaging them, and gasped in pain.

She found that it was his detached attitude that upset her the most, even in violence he was detached, as if doing a job, just another job about the home, going through motions, and that, she now realized, was how he saw her, and how he had seen her all along. He didn't see her as a person, she was a component in the machine called 'the farm', she had her place, her function, like an animal in a stall. And the richest thing of all, she thought, is that it wasn't her fault that he'd lost half a day yesterday because he'd been stupid enough to point out a freshly dug grave to the police. It wasn't her fault that he didn't keep his mouth shut, didn't just let the police stand by in ignorance until the owner came and collected his car.

'I don't want to be unhelpful but there really isn't such a profile. Not to my knowledge.'

'No?' Abernethy trapped the 'phone between his ear and shoulder while he held his pen poised to write.

'I'm afraid not. People abduct children for a host of reasons.' Cass spoke confidently and with authority. Abernethy felt soothed by his voice. 'It isn't as though a profile of a child abductor exists in much the same way as the profile of the serial killer exists. Really, your guess is as good as mine . . . I can't give you much time, I'm teaching in ten minutes, but suspect the obvious . . . I mean, a household with healthy happy children is unlikely to be the domicile of a person who abducted this little boy . . . it is the little boy mentioned in this morning's *Herald*, I assume?'

'Yes, sir, the very one.'

'I feel for his parents. But look for a single person: probably a woman, but not necessarily so—it's just that women have stronger need for a child than a man, consider perhaps two people acting in consent as in Hindley and Brady.'

Abernethy felt a chill shoot down his spine.

'There just isn't a model,' Cass continued and Abernethy had the impression he was struggling. 'The likely culprit could be anyone from a woman who has a desperate need for a child and in whose custody, unlawful as it may be, the child will be safe and unharmed to a male pædophile with rape and murder on his mind. I really can't help. I would advise you to ask other children rather than adults, on the basis that they too might have been approached, but that's common sense rather than applied psychology. I can't be of further help, Mr Abernethy.'

'Thanks anyway, Dr Cass.' Abernethy replaced the handset gently.

'I'm embarrassed,' he said. He did not think that the 'phone call did the street credibility of the police any good at all. 'I just don't think that the 'phone call did our street cred any good. Any good at all.'

'What did he say?'

Abernethy told her.

'Common sense, really,' conceded Elka Willems. 'Still, what Fabian wants, Fabian gets. Let's go knock on a few doors.'

'It was about here, sir.' Sussock stood at the side of a narrow road. 'I was here for about two hours. It's a little different from how I remember it but this is the place all right.' Sussock carried his jacket under his arm. Donoghue, walking behind him, kept his jacket on despite the heat. Six uniformed officers, a dog-handler and a sergeant stood by.

'Where are we from the location at which the body was found yesterday, Ray?' Donoghue loosened the knot in his tie. His one concession to the heat.

'About a mile from here, sir, I should think. Same sort of country, narrow roads, fields, farming country.'

'So twenty-five years ago the stolen vehicle was found here?'

'Just where we are standing, sir.'

'And the toy rabbit?'

'Along there, by the shrubs. Same side of the road that the car was on.'

'So if there is a body about here, and it is buried in the same relative position to where the car was parked and the rabbit dropped as the relative position to the car and rabbit yesterday, where would it be?'

'In this field here, sir.' Sussock nodded to a field of rough, uneven pasture.

'It wouldn't be too far from the car anyway.' Donoghue pondered. 'I'm assuming that the car was used to carry the body to the field for burial and once here it would be a dead weight, literally.'

'Why leave the car, though?' Sussock shook his head. 'It would make more sense to use it to make good his escape.'

'That's a good point, Ray. I confess I've thought about it and the only deduction I can make is that we are not dealing with a rational mind. We'll observe the procedures, but I can say now that if the girl in the GRI is Sandra Shapiro, all her known associates, even her enemies, will be able to account for themselves at the time of her disappearance, and at the assumed time of her death.' Donoghue turned to the uniformed officer. 'Sergeant.'

'Sir!'

'This field here. Not all of it, I would say no more than fifty feet from the fence.'

'Very good, sir. We'll let the dog go first.'

'As you see fit.'

The sergeant nodded to the dog-handler, who led the Alsatian to the edge of the field and slipped the leash. The animal swept over the fencing, as sleek and lithe as a puma, and began to criss-cross the field, snout down.

It found nothing.

'I'm sorry, sir.' The dog-handler seemed to feel himself to be personally responsible, personally at fault. He slipped the leash back on the animal and patted its flank. 'But after twenty-five years . . . you see, they smell decaying flesh all right but . . .'

'It was worth a try,' said Donoghue and again turned to the sergeant. 'It's got to be spadework I'm afraid, Sergeant. If you'd form a file, say about four feet apart, dig once over two feet down to . . . How deep was the grave yesterday, Ray?'

'Ten inches should do it, sir.'

'Ten inches, a depth of ten inches, please.'

'Very good, sir.' The sergeant addressed the group of constables. 'Right, lads, grab a spade, we'll be on this for the rest of the morning and into the afternoon, I'd say, so let's take it steady. Pace yourselves.'

They paced themselves for forty-five minutes until a young constable drove his spade vertically into the soil and found that the expected resistance wasn't there. The spade slid deeply into unconsolidated earth. He dug further. He encountered a rock which dislodged easily. Under the rock was a bone. A human bone.

CHAPTER 5

Friday, 14.00–23.30 hours

'It appears that the fair fields of Lanarkshire are giving up their dead.' Reynolds crouched beside the shallow grave and considered the skeleton, hunched in the foetal position, on its side, hands tied behind the back.

Donoghue stood behind and beside Reynolds. Both men were concealed by a screen which had been hastily erected as soon as the first of the bones had been exposed. 'It so appears,' he said.

'Do you think that the two murders are connected?'

'Sir? Two murders.'

'I mean this one and the girl found yesterday.'

'Possibly,' Donoghue conceded. 'Our minds are open to every possibility. Can you perhaps tell me why you ask?'

Reynolds stood and brushed soil from his hands. 'Well, over and above the fact that they're both buried in the same overall location, not above a mile apart, I should say they're both with hands tied and in the foetal position, and both young women.'

'How can you tell us that?'

'Shape of the pelvis and the wide orbits of the eye cavity in the skull.' Reynolds spoke matter of factly. 'They confirm that this is a skeleton of an adult human female. The skull hadn't fully knitted by the time of death, so we have a skeleton of someone, some girl, between the ages of sixteen and twenty when she died. It's been buried a long time though, putrification is complete, very little flesh, she's been here for twenty years, perhaps. Perhaps nearer thirty.'

'We think twenty-five, sir,' said Donoghue.

Reynolds nodded. 'So, they are connected, you think? Despite the time-gap.'

'Yes.' Donoghue nodded. 'We do in fact believe there's a connection. Don't know what or who as yet but the two bodies constitute a single line of inquiry.'

'I find that a little unsettling.' Reynolds glanced up and over the top of the screen at the rolling hills about him, cattle grazing, mountains in the distance, woodland interrupting the skyline. 'I mean, what else has happened in the twenty-five-year interval? How many more skeletons are in these fields?'

'I confess that that has occurred to us, sir.'

'I'm sure it has.' Reynolds looked downwards again. He looked particularly at the stones beside the excavation. 'Tell me, did you find these stones on top of the body?'

'Yes, and inside the skeleton too, but not completely covering it.'

'The stones would have fallen into the skeleton, as you say, into the chest cavity and thighs as the flesh decomposed. That's why you found them mixed up with the bones, but they would have been placed on top of the body. You know, he had more time to bury this victim.'

'Oh.'

'I would assume that the stones were put on the body to prevent foxes digging it up. He didn't do that with the body we found yesterday. It never occurred to him to do it yesterday, or he hadn't the time, or as the years have taken their toll on him, as years take toll on us all, then carrying the body, digging the grave and covering it, took all the stamina he could muster. He no longer had the stamina to collect and carry stones. But a quarter of a century ago he would have been a different man. I wonder, too,' he continued, 'just thinking aloud, you understand, whether he has some connection with the sea?'

'How do you mean, sir?'

'Well, yesterday the post-mortem revealed that the victim had died in a saline solution of three per cent, which at first I took to have been sea-water. Now, these rocks, note them, anything strike you about them?'

Donoghue confessed they looked like ordinary rocks to him.

'Ever noticed the difference between stones on the shore and stones inland?'

Donoghue saw it then. The rocks that had been placed on top of the body were rounded, large pebbles. 'Sea action,' he said.

'Wave action, I think is the term,' said Reynolds. 'These rocks have been taken from a coastal location. Rocks dug up from the fields would be jagged. It may be a red herring, it may be that if he wanted rocks in a hurry he thought— probably correctly—that he'd be quicker driving down to the coast and picking them up from the shore than he would be digging them out of the ground. But equally it may indicate where he lives.'

'It's worth considering,' said Donoghue. 'Might also be an attempt to throw us off the scent, like salting the drowning fluid.'

'If that was deliberate. It may be an accidental indication.' Reynolds turned to Donoghue.

'Of?'

'Of the sex of the perpetrator. This is something else that occurred to me last night. I'm just bouncing it off you, but supposing that the victim drowned in a bath, as opposed to another large container, and supposing that the water in which she drowned was not drawn for the purpose but was left over from a person having bathed, that is, using the container for the purpose for which it was intended, then what reason would one have for salting the bathwater?'

'I haven't a clue.'

'Cystitis, Mr Donoghue, cystitis, suffered by women, it's

an infection of the urethra and/or bladder. Women have to live with it, but doctors often advise salting bathwater as a means of easing the discomfort. I'd have to say that three per cent salinity is a high concentration. For that purpose, doctors normally advise sufferers to sprinkle a handful of salt into the bathwater, which would be much less than three per cent volume in a normal bath, but if the woman concerned is suffering acutely from it, or if she is over-fastidious—'

'The point is that the perpetrator might be a woman.'

'Or a woman is involved, because the carrying of the body over the fence and into the field and the digging of the grave in a single night took real stamina. A very well-built woman could have done it, though.'

'But it's given us something to consider.'

'Or just confused everything?' The silver-haired pathologist smiled. 'Tell me this, this skeleton here, was this the reason why yesterday, you asked if it was possible to identify a skull?'

'It was.' Donoghue nodded. 'It was indeed. We had a notion that this might be the case.'

King drove down the Gallowgate, down a canyon of black tenements, turned into Westmuir Street, factories, waste ground, Shettleston Road, shops, pubs, more black tenements, mixed in with new developments. He turned right at Shettleston Sheddings and entered Egypt.

The house was classic Egypt, city-owned, semi-detached, whitewashed, glinting in the afternoon, lawns clipped low and neat, pink roses growing on the trellis by the door. The street was narrow and quiet. A few cars, polished, neatly parked. Pure Egypt: a pocket of squeaky clean in the sprawling East End.

The inside of the house, King found, presented the same obsessive neatness and cleanliness as the outside, everything in its place, but suffered from a lack of imagination and had the unmistakable stamp of a tight budget over the years.

The man had stood and looked at King, and King had observed the look in the man's eyes as emotion vacated to make way for shock as the latter eased into the man's mind. The man who had opened the door at King's polite but insistent knock, who stood on his threshold in a blue shirt and cream slacks, a gold watch on a thin arm, had looked questioningly at King and then, concerned as King flashed his ID, now stood reacting inwardly from shock. The man never showed any sense of fear, no sense of guilt, no hostility: King saw and recognized the sort of household he was paid to protect.

The man had stepped backwards, had said yes, yes, of course he could come in, and as he did so he called to his wife, 'Jessie, Jessie.' King had followed the man and walked into a house that had been recently dusted and sprayed with air-freshener, and moments later the woman sat sobbing on the settee as the man stood, his hand on her shoulder, and remained standing even as a little moisture crept into the corner of his eye.

'There's no mistake, I'm afraid.' King spoke slowly, with due gravity. He didn't elaborate, he hoped that Mr and Mrs Shapiro, houseproud, of Glenalmond Street, Egypt, didn't press him, did not ask how he was certain there could be no mistake. He would then have been obliged to tell them about her fingerprints being on file and about the convictions for soliciting as a common prostitute which led to her prints being recorded. It would do little good for them to find out now. 'There's no mistake,' he said again. He found that this was an aspect of police work which never got easier.

'What happened, sir?'

'Mr King,' said King, who hated being called 'sir' by

men old enough to be his father. 'My name's King. I'm afraid to tell you, sir, that we believe your daughter to have been murdered. That is as yet unproven, but we believe it to be the case.'

'Oh . . .' Mr Shapiro collapsed on to the settee next to his wife in a single fluid movement, like a statue suddenly turning to jelly. King turned his head. Embarrassed, uncomfortable, he glanced out of the net curtains as a summer breeze entered the open window, fluttered the curtains, and let them fall again. A car, polished and clean, drove slowly down Glenalmond Street, its windscreen and chrome catching the sun as it passed. King turned away from the window. Inside the Shapiros' home a budgerigar twittered from within its cage and a row of little glass animals marched across the mantelpiece. On the settee a middle-aged couple sat and gripped each other with trembling hands, the woman sobbing uncontrollably, unashamedly.

'What happened, sir? Mr King. What happened?'

'Well . . .' King indicated the vacant armchair, good solid quality, but worn, the sort of item of furniture which had been purchased in the early days, the hopeful days, the it'll-cost-but-it'll-see-us-out-days. 'Do you mind if . . . ?'

'No . . . please do, Mr King.'

King sat thankfully. He thought it bad enough to bring news to their door like the news he had brought: he didn't have to stand towering over them as well.

'Can we see her?' Mrs Shapiro seemed to be in a world of her own, King thought that she hadn't heard her husband's question.

'Yes,' said King, taking the woman's question first and head on. 'Yes, you have the right to view her, but I'd advise against it because it will be the way you will remember her. I'm led to believe that the final image of her will live in your mind more than any other image or memory. You may want to preserve some happier memory . . .'

'What happened, sir?' Mr Shapiro pressed.

'We believe that she was drowned, sir,' said King gently.

'Drowned?'

King nodded. 'Death was due to drowning, but beyond that there are indications of suspicious circumstances, which is why I am obliged to tell you that we believe she was drowned. Rather than simply drowned. Our inquiries are far from complete so I can say little else. That is why . . . that is my second reason for calling.'

Mr Shapiro nodded. The essence of his character seemed to King to be one of deference.

'I was to break the tragic news of Sandra's death, sir, and also to ask for information about her. As much as you can tell us.'

'Anything we can tell you, sir.'

King opened his book. 'You won't object if I take notes as we speak?'

'Not at all, sir.'

King looked at him. 'You really don't have to call me "sir", sir.'

Mr Shapiro nodded. Mrs Shapiro suddenly stood and ran from the room into the kitchen, pushing her face into a handkerchief as she did so.

'Mrs Shapiro has a problem with her nerves,' said the man. 'She's not so well able to contain her emotions at the best of times, at a time like this . . .'

'There's no need for apologies, sir.' King held up his hand. 'Please, really.'

The man nodded and smiled briefly with tightly clenched lips.

'Your daughter, sir,' King prodded.

'Our only child,' said Mr Shapiro. 'Just a few days short of her twentieth birthday. She had drifted away from us in the last year or two. Ours was a blissful family life for the first twelve, fourteen years. I had regular employment. I work for the transport executive, I drive a bus, the forty-one, City Centre to Easterhouse and back. I can drive the route blindfolded. Our Sandra was a bonny wee girl, made our life so full. Do you know that in those fourteen years the only crisis we had was Mrs Shapiro's emergency appendix operation?' He shook his head as if in wonderment.

'There's not many families that can say that,' said King, as he gently slid his hand on to the wooden arm of the chair, hoping that the man didn't see the small observation of a superstition. His own family life was full, his own cup runneth over, he had a blissful marriage to a beautiful Quaker woman, a lovely, lovely young boy, and as so often in his work, his visit to the Shapiros' had forced him to confront the fact that it could all be taken from him in an instant. He knew that he would return home that night, that he would slide into bed and hold Rosemary even if she was sleeping, and that tomorrow he would roll around on the floor with Iain, that they would build a pile of coloured plastic bricks together, and he'd do that because they were alive and his. And if that meant that Rosemary's shelves didn't get put up, then they didn't get put up because one day she and Iain might be late getting home and instead of them he would open the door to a cop, maybe one of his colleagues, who would say, 'Richard . . .' He took his hand from the wood of the armchair and held the pen over his pad.

'Then, as many girls do, Sandra started flapping her wings when she got to be about fifteen or so.'

'Normal,' said King. 'Normal and healthy.'

'Aye, so we told ourselves, but looking back it was the end of our family, the end of the blissful period, see, her and Mrs Shapiro fighting like two alley cats. This is a quiet area, Mr King, as you'll notice. I'm still embarrassed about the noise they made, spilled out into the street once, screaming at each other. Then when she was seventeen she announced that she was leaving home. All right, hen, we said. If that's what you want, then go, but remember that this is home, this is where you belong. Come back any time, even if it's just for a feed. See, me, I know how teenagers in bedsits neglect themselves, so I do.'

'I know what you mean,' said King.

'Probably more than me. Drowned you say?'

King nodded.

'We knew she'd been reported as a missing person, sir, a policewoman came to the door. She told us, asked us if we knew of her whereabouts, took details and a photograph we had of her. That was about a week ago, we've been fretting ever since. When I saw you, I was upstairs, I watched you park your car, I watched you get out, I knew that you were a policeman, you have that manner about you, Mr King, even in plain clothes, it's like a uniform in a way, neat, well turned out, if I may say so, and you carry yourself in a self-assured manner and as if you are saying by your manner "I know something that you don't know".'

'Being that I am a policeman.'

'Aye, you may, I've been driving a bus now for twenty years. I drive the East End schemes, I told you, and often I see a man dressed like you, neatly, and he'll be tall, healthy-looking and he'll be among all the overgrown gardens and burnt-out cars and houses with metal sheets over the windows and pale-looking people who don't have enough clothing in the bad weather and I'll clock him and say "police". Often there are two of them. You stick out like sore thumbs, really.'

'It's not a question of us hiding our identity,' said King, who knew well that the police could blend and merge if necessary. He had once had occasion to visit Easterhouse police station in the early hours of the morning, about 3.0 a.m., he recalled, and was standing chatting to the uniform bar officer when a man walked in off the street, long hair, ragged beard, torn denims, dirty training shoes, the man walked past the uniform bar and through the door marked CID. 'Drug Squad,' the bar officer had said, 'they're here for the next week or two. There's a big turn going down, strictly need to know only.'

King asked Mr Shapiro for his daughter's address.

'I gave it to the other officer, the lady constable.'

'I didn't take a note of it.' It was a diplomatic answer, the truth being that the only address in the MP file was Glenalmond Road, Egypt. It was poor attention to detail on the part of the interested constable.

Mr Shapiro gave King an address in Hillhead. Cecil Street, Hillhead.

'When did you last see her, sir?'

'About ten days ago now, she came to see us, 'phoned us the day before, told us she'd be visiting for an evening meal, which she did, a salad, cold ham and a sweet. She stayed, late for her, stayed until nine-thirty. Funny how little details stick. I remember the conversation word for word. I walked her to the bus stop on the corner and she caught a bus to the town. She said she'd call and see us next week. Three days after that the lady constable knocked on our door. I told Mrs Shapiro that it would be all right but in myself . . . You know, I find it a strange relief that you've called. I watched you park your motor and I said to myself, "Thank the Lord Jesus, the waiting's over."'

King paused. The man was lost in thought. The clock ticked. The budgerigar sang, a car drove past. Eventually King said, 'What did Sandra do for a living, sir?' though really King knew that a more accurate question would be, 'What did she tell you she did for a living?'

'She worked in a baker's shop. A confectioner's.'

It was easily verified. King wondered if perhaps the nocturnal activity for which she fetched up in the District Court was a sideline, a bit of spending money. But it had been

King's long-held observation that a girl would go on to the streets to ease financial hardship, intending to do so for a brief period, but instead she would find herself on a downward spiral and the street would rapidly become her primary source of income. Especially when she found that a few hours on the street would provide her with as much money as she would earn in a few weeks working in a shop. She might even get hooked on the adrenalin, and the camaraderie that exists among the girls. The drawback of the life is that if they survive the STDs, they may end up in a shallow grave in a field in Lanarkshire.

'Any idea of her friends, her social life?'

The man shook his head. 'No. She wouldn't tell us. We know that she had lost all contact with her school chums.'

'Did you visit her flat?'

'She wouldn't let us.'

King nodded. 'Striking out on her own.'

The door to the kitchen creaked open. Mrs Shapiro entered the room. 'I want to see her,' she said. 'I want to see her now.' Her jaw was firm, her tone resolute. King saw no trace of emotion in her demeanour, save perhaps for determination.

'If you wish.' King realized that she would not be persuaded otherwise, and it was her full and complete right to view the body of her daughter.

'I'll get my jacket.' Mr Shapiro stood and left the room.

'This is not a surprise to us.' The woman spoke without looking at King. 'I knew, as only a mother can. I think Sandy did too, but we didn't tell each other. We pretended for the sake of each other.'

King stood. 'I'd like to make a 'phone call,' he said. 'To the GRI, let them know we are on our way.'

'In the hall, sir. Bottom of the stairs.'

King went into the hallway and picked up the 'phone. It

was a bright red appliance, glaringly out of place among the polished wood, sober carpet and green plants.

It was a procedure which never reduced in its solemnity, even for the cops and the nurses for whom it was a necessary part of the normal working day.

There was first the hum and buzz of activity of the central rotunda in the GRI. Then the descent to the basement down a spiral staircase during which any noise of the hospital is left very rapidly behind, as if even another, much more sober world is being entered. It is also at this point that all conversation between relatives, police, and medical staff cease. From the point that the central rotunda is left behind the party walks in silence until moments before the viewing. There is then a long walk down a corridor, a corridor with central heating pipes running along the roof, doors set back and with yellow triangular radiation warning notices on them. A door is reached, another corridor is entered, this corridor is prefabricated and runs on the outside of the main building. It has a floor of black rubber matting and assumes a gentle decline. It bends at a sharp angle and continues on to a heavy door. King opened the door and the Shapiros entered in dumb shock; each, thought King, would be clinging to a shred of hope of some awful fortunate mistake having been made, a mistake that would mean their daughter might yet be alive. A senior nursing sister stood gravely beside a screen over which a heavy blue tapestry was draped. A golden cord hung beside the tapestry. Upholstered seats ran round the walls of the room. A low light burned.

'Have you done this before?' asked the sister.

'No, miss.' Mr Shapiro spoke.

'She was a good girl.' Mrs Shapiro shook her head, fighting back the tears.

'It's different to the way you might have seen it done on

television.' The nurse spoke with authority and deference.
'The curtain will be drawn and you will view the deceased
through a pane of glass.'

'I see,' said Mr Shapiro.

'She will be lying on a trolley. You'll see only the face.
She has been bandaged at the scalp line and round the side
and back of her head and under the chin.

'Yes, miss.'

'She has been washed. You won't see any injuries. It will
be as if looking at her when she's sleeping.'

The Shapiros nodded.

'If you'd like to take a seat.'

King and Shapiro sat on the bench. The nursing sister
left the room via a door beside the golden thread.

All was silence. King moved and caused the plastic
upholstery to squeak, after which he resisted all further
urges to move. Minutes elapsed and then a trolley was
heard being moved into position behind the glass behind
the tapestry.

Silence.

A brief period of silence. The door opened, the nursing
sister stood in the room. She paused and then began to pull
the cord, the tapestry began to lift, and as one the Shapiros
stood and walked to the glass. King waited a moment and
then he too stood as if drawn to the glass. He looked down
at a face he had only previously seen in a photograph, a
girl, attractive, eyes closed, as if indeed she was sleeping on
a trolley beneath tightly tucked blankets. Her face white,
white, white.

Nobody else was in sight, the lighting of the room was
such that nothing beyond the trolley could be seen. It was
as if the girl was lying suspended, devoid of any material
environment.

Mrs Shapiro collapsed on her husband's shoulder. The
nursing sister closed the curtain, all in silence.

'Thank you, miss,' said Mr Shapiro.

'Thank you,' said Mrs Shapiro. 'I wanted to see her. I mean had to. Without seeing her I just would not have believed that she was dead.'

King nodded his thanks to the nursing sister and then turned to the Shapiros. 'I'll take you home.'

No. It never, ever, got easier. And the day it was easy, the day he did this and felt nothing, that day would be the last day he would serve as a police officer.

She sat in the chair. She surveyed the room. The room she had grown up in. They were here somewhere in the room.

They had to be.

She had to find them. Before she fed him. That's it, he would get food, no water, not until she found them. Her spare spectacles.

She had done this before. It was like waking up after a dream.

A dream that can last for days. The spectacles were all right on Wednesday. She saw the girl then. Now it's Friday. She couldn't remember what happened after she saw the girl to take her photograph.

People came and went in these times. The girl had gone, but now she had a boy in the cupboard. She didn't know why the girl had left, she had liked her. She didn't know where her spectacles were. She had to find the spare pair. Then she'd feed the boy. Just a little.

She'd get by until the optician could see her. Just use the left-hand fork to stab the left-hand piece of meat, the right hand to pick up the right-hand cup. Not difficult. Or keep the patch on.

Can't drive, though. Can't do that. Have to find the spare pair or wait for a new pair before she could drive.

*

'Oh, the little boy,' said the woman with obvious sincerity and concern, after Abernethy and Willems had shown their ID and explained their purpose.

'You know something?' asked Elka Willems.

'Only what I've heard, and what I've read in the papers. That poor woman and her husband, I wish I'd seen something. I have children of my own.'

'If you hear of anything, anything at all,' said Abernethy, feeling his hopes dashed again, 'please contact us.'

The door shut behind them and they turned towards the gate and the leafy Broomhill Avenue.

'Just got to keep going,' said Abernethy.

'All we can.' Elka Willems smiled. 'It's all we can do.'

Donoghue sat in his office. He glanced up and to his side, at the people milling in Sauchiehall Street. It was the homeward rush hour, which as usual had begun earlier than on the previous days of the working week. It was 4.30 p.m. and the rush hour was already in full flow. The downtown bars would be filling and not a few wouldn't make it home tonight, not without help anyway.

Somewhere out there was a man. He had abducted a woman, held her captive, then drowned her and then buried her in a field.

And he had done the same thing twenty-five years ago.

And he may have done the same thing any number of times in the intervening period. And maybe even before that. There was no way of telling if the skeleton found that early afternoon was his first victim.

He returned his gaze to his desktop; by that stage of the day, a shifting sand of files and papers and memos. He excavated his telephone, dialled nine for an outside line and then an Edinburgh number. 'It's me,' he said when his call was answered. He heard his children squabbling in the background.

'Just get home asap,' said a woman's voice. 'I'm at my wits' end, I'm at the end of my tether. I'm reduced to threats now and that's not working, we need the calm controlling fatherly—'

'That's what I'm 'phoning for.'

'Oh . . . you're not going to be late . . . of all the days to pick. I'm pulling my hair out here . . .'

'And I'll be working tomorrow. And maybe even Sun . . .'

'Fabian . . .' Pleadingly. Then his wife's voice hardened. 'Well, at least you can speak to them . . .' She put the 'phone down hard on the cabinet and he heard her calling out. 'Timothy, Louise . . . your father wants to speak to you. Now. I said now!'

Bothwell scratched his head as he considered the car. It was a green Ford Escort, four-door, about two years old going by the registration. He took the squirrel-hair brush and began to dust the steering-wheel for fingerprints, knowing that the car had been driven away from the locus only after a second wheel had been braced over the steering-wheel to prevent the police driver smudging latents. A quick delicate dusting with fine iron powder revealed a series of smudges which could only have been made by a gloved hand. There was little point, he reasoned, in dusting for prints when the perpetrator had clearly worn gloves; who else, he thought, would wear gloves to drive a car in the middle of summer? He replaced the brush and began to go over the car inch by inch, bagging and tagging everything that he found. It was Friday, already beyond the end of his working day. He had an elderly mother with whom he shared a modest tenement in Queens Park whom he knew would fret if he was not at home on time. He had an obligation to attend a committee meeting of the Bowling Club that evening and began to doubt that he would be finished in time to attend. He put both nagging annoyances to the back of his mind and set to work diligently, methodically and slowly. By 19.30 he felt that he had searched the car minutely. He had bagged and tagged a number of items but would in his report bring special attention to:

(1) strands of human hair
(2) coarse tufts of fabric as from a carpet
(3) a lens as from a pair of spectacles.

He also noted in his report that the last person to drive the car appeared to have worn gloves. He added that he hoped the information would be of use. He signed his report in a large round hand—E. Bothwell.

He submitted his report, as yet still handwritten, to the internal mail system FTAO Inspector Donoghue, P. Division, Charing Cross. He then made two 'phone calls; first home to his anxiety-ridden parent, yes, yes, he was quite safe, just had to work late. Home in an hour. The second to the secretary of the Bowling Club, and transmitted his apologies for his absence owing to unforeseen obligations at his place of employment.

He left the premises. It was a calm, pleasant evening, warm still air and high cloud. He decided to walk home. Why not? He got little exercise these days.

'It's going to mean late working.' Donoghue lit his pipe. 'I know it's Friday evening. Richard, you're on duty anyway, but WPC Williams and DC Abernethy, you're day shift. I'd like you to hang on a wee while longer.' Abernethy and Williams nodded. A 'wee while': Abernethy thought that to be a little rich. His shift had finished at 14.00. It was already close to 20.00, a wee six hours longer already.

'It may be that you can't get home at a reasonable time, but we have two major inquiries at the present and as usual we are understaffed. I'll be coming in tomorrow so rank has no privileges.' He paused, took his pipe from his mouth and placed it in the ashtray. 'Two major inquiries pressing. I received a report from Bothwell just before you came in, he's taken a few items from the car and sent them to Dr Kay. She's giving up her Friday evening to help us, so we must not appear to be idle. So let's see where we are: WPC Willems, anything on the house-to-house in respect of Tim Moore?'

'Nothing, sir.' Elka Willems shuffled in her seat. 'But in instances like this, all we can say is "nothing yet". People's memories sometimes have a delayed reaction.'

'Agreed.' Donoghue nodded. 'We can still hope that you and Abernethy might have triggered something. What's the next step?'

'Enlist the help of the media, sir,' Abernethy said hesitatingly. 'Run off the MP posters we have mocked up, ask the newspapers to print it. Get it shown on television. Blanket coverage, go nationwide, police stations, bus stations, railway stations, London Underground. I can get on to that this evening.'

'Good man.' Donoghue drummed his fingers on the desktop. 'Richard.'

'Sir?'

'Your plans?'

'Continuing with Sandra Shapiro inquiry. I intend to visit her flat in Hillhead. I'll do that this evening.'

'Good. WPC Willems, if you'll assist Abernethy with the posters. Tomorrow, Abernethy, tomorrow I'd like you to go round the toy shops.'

'Sir?'

'The furry rabbit found at the locus of Sandra Shapiro's grave. We must try to identify the outlet. Take it out of productions and go down Argyle Street and Sauchiehall Street tomorrow. A retailer might be able to identify it. It's a long shot but it might tell us something.'

'Very good, sir.'

'Meanwhile we won't wait with bated breath for anything that Dr Kay can tell us. Any points that I've missed?'

'Was there a spade in the car, sir?'

'No.' Donoghue shook his head and then saw what King was driving at. 'No, Bothwell made no mention of it, but you're right, he didn't dig the grave with his bare hands.'

'Light's all but gone.' King glanced out of the window. 'Not enough daylight left, not by the time we get out there.'

'But somewhere there's a spade or a pick or similar. And someone may have seen the murderer walk from the field and leave the area.'

'Second car or public transport?'

Donoghue shook his head. 'Either, though a second car would imply a conspirator. Somehow I think that that is unlikely. There was no reason why the first car wasn't used to escape, no reason that I can see, and that's a puzzle in itself. On balance my guess would be public transport. If you'd get on to that, Richard.'

'Tomorrow, sir, first thing.'

Pippa Scott was naked. Malcolm Montgomerie was naked. The flame behind them was naked; a candle burning in a metal tray on a low table. Also on the table were empty plates, a bottle of wine and two wine glasses.

'It's better this way,' she said, nestled back against his chest. 'I prefer it. Do it first and eat and drink afterwards. If you wine and dine first you dull the sensations.'

He had picked her up from school. He had watched her as she walked away from the building, a beautiful carriage, her long hair about her shoulders. She was a woman whom Montgomerie had found had benefited from a privileged education at one of the most prestigious public schools in England, but whose socialist convictions and family connections with Scotland had brought her to teach in Govan, and it was on that level that they had reached each other. He had given up a promising career in the law, he had felt ill at ease with the smug, self-satisfied undergraduates in the Faculty of Law at Edinburgh University: young men who said things like, 'I did law because you never meet a poor solicitor,' and who scoffed at his idea of being a 'people's lawyer'. He left after his first year, returned to his native Glasgow and volunteered for the police. Montgomerie found Pippa Scott to be a strongly confident young woman, handsome in a very feminine way, who had taken him by surprise on their first date by pushing his glass of Grappa towards him at the end of the meal and saying, 'Drink up if we're going to sleep together tonight.' They did, a little clumsily, being unused to each other's bodies, but not at all unsuccessfully.

She had friends in teaching whom he liked. She had friends in the media, on the strength of a few scripts for a soap opera, whom he didn't like. He felt they had smirked when he had to apologize for leaving the soirée early, to go on duty.

That evening he had driven to Govan to pick her up and returned with her to her flat on Hyndland. Afterwards they had bathed together and she pampered him with herbal shampoo.

King climbed the common stair. The building was dark and damp. Even now, in midsummer, it was dark and damp. They were narrow stairs, worn down with age, winding in a high spiral, with rusted railings which seemed too frail to be able to withstand human weight. The stairs of the tenement seemed to King to be straining on the verge of collapse. Many of the doors had Asian surnames written on them, some hastily scribbled with pen on a scrap of paper and Sellotaped to the door, or pencilled on the flaking plaster beside the door. Others had names embossed on plastic nameplates. The stair was filled with the smell of curry and Indian music, monotonous to King's ears. At the top of the stair, on a landing of uneven flagstones beneath a dirty skylight which had been meshed over with chicken wire, were two doors. One was locked with a padlock and hasp and did not appear to King to have been opened for some months, if not years. By the side of the second door a sheet of A4 paper had been Sellotaped to the wall. Ten names had been written on the paper. Some had been scored out. One name was Shapiro. It was also one of the names with a decisive pencil line running through it. King wondered if she had quit the address some time earlier and not informed her parents. Or perhaps someone reading of her death in the newspaper had crossed her name off the list in a callous gesture of dismissiveness and thoughtlessness for any next of kin who might want to collect her possessions.

King rapped on the door. The sound echoed down the stair.

No reply.

He knocked again, harder.

The door was opened eventually and uninterestedly. A girl, early twenties, thought King, lost-looking, bleary-eyed, stood in the doorway, one hand on the door, the other on the frame. 'What?'

'Police.' King flashed his ID.

'So?'

'I'd like to come in.'

She began to shut the door.

King pushed it open and stepped into the hall. It was dimly lit, cluttered with bric-à-brac and piles of old newspapers.

'You got a warrant?'

'Do I need one? Have you got something to hide?'

'Hasn't everybody?'

'Tell me about Sandra Shapiro.'

'The late Sandra Shapiro. I read the papers, *Evening Times* early edition, read it today, so I scored her name from the list of names on the door. There's only me here now.'

'So who are all those names on the door?'

'Some of them are made up. Keeps the burglars out. One or two are there as mail drops for drifters with no fixed abode, as I believe is the phrase. Others are mail drops for guys on the run from the law. Anyway, I read about Sandra so I crossed her name off the list.'

'Considerate of you.'

'She wasn't anything to me. She was just a girl who had a room here, she was a wee turk with an attitude.'

'Oh?'

'She came, she went, she lifted anything that wasn't nailed down and now she's dead.'

'So what's your name?'

'Do I need to tell you?'

King remained silent.

'Valerie Lambie. I was a nurse and now I'm not.'

'Probably a good job, with your attitude.'

'What's that supposed to mean?'

'You can take that any way you like, Valerie Lambie. Which is Sandra's room?'

Valerie Lambie nodded over her left shoulder. As she did so King caught a glimpse of track marks in her neck.

'Did Sandra shoot up too?'

Valerie Lambie's hand went up to her neck. She shrugged her shoulders. 'It's the only place I've got veins left. I'm not proud. I'm not apologetic either. Sandra?' The girl shook her head. 'No, I don't think she did, but she was on her way there. She'd watch me shoot up and you could see the fascination in her eyes. If she hadn't been topped she would have been a smackhead in a matter of weeks, days maybe, I don't know.'

King stepped towards the door to Sandra Shapiro's room. He pressed it. It was locked. He put his shoulder to it and nudged it open. The small lock in rotten wood offered no resistance.

'I have a key for it,' said Valerie Lambie with a sneer as King examined the damage to the wooden frame. 'All you had to do was ask.'

King ignored her and turned his attention to Sandra Shapiro's room. He was too experienced to be goaded into police brutality by Valerie Lambie, but the possibility of a compulsory detoxification by means of a bust for possession began to loom as a very interesting prospect.

Sandra Shapiro's room was small, a bed, a wardrobe, a threadbare carpet, a grimy window. King stepped up to the window: it looked out on a back court of sheer-sided black tenements, tipped-over dustbins, cats on the walls menacing each other. He stepped back and opened the wardrobe. Sandra Shapiro's clothes were old and tattered.

'It went on the drink.' Valerie Lambie stood in the doorway.

'Sorry?'

'Her money. That's what you are thinking, isn't it? Are you or are you not standing there thinking to your little self, where, oh where, did all her dosh go? Well, it went on the drink. When she came here she was on the vodka, a refined taste too, only blue label was good enough for her. By the time she'd been here for a couple of months she was into the Thunderbirds, the Buckfasts, you name it, her head was blown apart and her brains had been clawed out. She was one step away from the hair lacquer and the brass polish. She was some mess. That's why I said I thought she was close to mainlining smack. See me, I'd rather be a smackhead than a crucial bevvy merchant like she was. See her sometimes, I'd go for a drink with her, she'd persuade me and if I was fed up with my own company I'd go, and pretty soon she'd sort of leer at me, she only ever needed topping up, you see, and she'd say things like, "Which pub are we in?" She was in the gutter all right.'

'She get her money on the street?'

'Are you asking or telling?'

'Both.'

'That's a contradiction, but yes, she worked the street. But not like I work the street, not every night winter and summer. She went down there twice a week, turned a few tricks until she had enough for a three-day bender. Then she'd come home with a brown paper bag full of bottles and cans and disappear into her room and she'd stagger out again three days later and go to the corner for a kebab. That was her food for the three days: a kebab. She'd spend a day recovering and then go back to the street for a couple of nights and earn enough for another carry-out. When she was working she could look quite smart, and it was at those times when she went to see her parents. They fed her a meal, and she said they'd see her off on the bus home. She was going home, but via the street.'

'Any friends?'

Valerie Lambie shook her head. Her sudden helpfulness, cynical as it may have been, had succeeded in making King rethink the heroin bust. He saw her as a victim. 'None to speak of,' she said. 'None in fact. Just winos, men and women with red faces and laser beams for breath. They'd come up in their droves when the word spread that she had been seen with a carry-out. Sometimes they got in, sometimes they didn't. That was Sandra Shapiro and now she's not.'

King left the flat, tripping lightly down the winding close and into Gibson Street. A group of students walked towards the University Union, an orange bus whined towards the city. He wondered if that was how one reacted against a dull, prim and unimaginative upbringing in Egypt. You leave and seek a gutter in any man's language. Maybe she drank because a chemical imbalance prevented her from resisting it; maybe Shapiro's house contained a dark secret and Sandra was fighting a deeply buried trauma? Whatever the reason, King was certain that the Shapiros did not need to see their only daughter's last resting-place save one.

Sussock sat in the deep armchair and looked about the room. An old wardrobe, a narrow divan bed, a small dark desk and then just enough room for the chair in which he sat, his long thin legs bent at the knee. There was a small window which looked out on to an elevated back lawn over which someone's washing hung in the still evening air. He watched a pair of swallows dive and spin: he heard a black-bird singing. All was quiet in the house, but only for the present. Later, when the pubs had shut, it would become noisy, later the boys whose floor was his ceiling would stamp home from the bar and switch on their hi-fi with the volume turned up to maximum and their music would boom-boom down into his boxroom. Through the wall, which wasn't a wall but a partition, he would soon hear the grunts of homosexual coupling, so close that it seemed as if he were in the same bed. That, he felt, was not too much of an exaggeration because when it came to it his bed and theirs were separated by a sheet of plywood about half an inch thick, if that, which had been covered in cheap wallpaper. The Polish landlord had divided up the huge rooms in the large old house in that manner, and as a consequence of the noise pollution the sense of personal space did not exist, except at times like this when it was quiet. In the room off the half-landing where the stair divided into two, the couple would doubtless soon be screaming either in orgasmic pleasure or murderous hatred: Sussock had noted that their emotions seemed to alternate nightly. Across the landing the young man who had been discharged and re-admitted and discharged from psychiatric hospitals as he wandered around Scotland, and who had by then fetched up in the same bedsitter address as Sussock, would be sitting on the edge of the bed, water pistol in hand, awaiting the Martians. He would sit there, fighting off sleep, sometimes for days, until he finally slumped backwards.

This was Sussock's home: he was a cop with thirty years' service, he was close to retirement, and this was his home.

He left his room and locked the door, it was not wholly secure, a grown man leaning on it could force the lock to give. He stepped lightly down the wide stairway and entered the small kitchen he shared with six or seven other residents. Somebody, he discovered, had taken his last can of beans, his last milk, his last teaspoonful of coffee. So he stole a teabag from somebody else's larder and some powdered milk from another person's foodstore. It was, he had found, how one survives in bedsit land. He sat in the kitchen sipping the tea. Adjacent to the kitchen was the landlord's lair and on one occasion Sussock had had call to go there to request a light bulb and he had seen how the man and his wife lived. He so lean and she so fat, like Jack Spratt and his wife. By day they lived in a room of upright chairs around a table, a sink under the window and a television on the draining-board. By night they evidently retired into a room which contained nothing but a double bed. They lived frugally, as if survival itself was a luxury, and they evidently expected their tenants to do the same. Sussock did not like them, he found them cold and distant and exploitative, they had a permanently resentful look about them and probably had a horrific tale of displaced persons and Nazi atrocities to tell, but no one could ever accuse them of hypocrisy. Not for them the Rolls-Royce and fabulous home of the traditional slum landlord; they lived in a basement with a television next to the sink.

Stealing himself for the ordeal he anticipated, he left the building and coaxed life into his old Ford. He drove to the south side, to Rutherglen, and stopped outside a prim bungalow. He noticed with a certain spiteful pleasure that the garden had grown wildly feral. Not coping, he said to himself. Not coping any more.

He left the car and walked to the side door of the building and hammered on it with the palm of his hand. It was opened slowly and eventually.

A young man stood there. He wore a black T-shirt, which he wore tucked into light trousers and open sandals. He had rings in both ears and wore his hair preened backwards. His hands were smooth and hairless. He held an embroidered handkerchief up to his face as he looked down at Sussock and smiled a transparently insincere smile. 'Daddy,' he said. 'We'd recognize that gentle tap on the door every time, Mummy and I.'

Sussock stormed up the steps and barged past his son.

'Get him out, Sammy.' A thin, highly pitched woman's voice shrieked from the dull recesses of the bungalow and Sussock pictured her sitting there in her chair, in the corner, small pinched face, scowling and demanding, demanding, demanding. 'Get him out, tell him to go and chase robbers, he was never any good to us, never here, always out, so tell him . . .'

Sussock ignored her, he ignored his sneering son. Earlier, in the immediate aftermath of leaving home, he would have been annoyed, provoked into violence perhaps, but no longer. Rummaging through his belongings for the summer coat and jacket he needed, he thought them both sad and very pathetic. And time would solve many things. His divorce would come through any day now and he could force an action for Division and Sale. Sell the bungalow, split the proceeds, that would give him enough for a room and kitchen of his own, from which no one could order him to go and where he could settle for a long and comfortable retirement.

Later, in the pub in Shawlands after a few beers and whiskies, he found himself brooding on the past. He still didn't know where things had gone wrong, he couldn't identify the point at which the rot had set in, and rot it was. His marriage had suffered a cancer which had grown insidiously and when the state of his marriage was recognized it was too late, the symptoms had been ignored for too long and when he did open up the body of his marriage, he had found it irredeemably riddled: shot to hell. Nothing to do but get out. A few months of difficult living conditions was, be believed, a small investment in order to earn a tranquil 'third phase' of life.

Last orders were called and Sussock edged to the end of the bar to make way for the inevitable stampede. He did not want more alcohol, he had drunk his fill, but even less he wanted to walk into the street. He caught the barman's attention and waved a five-pound note.

In the event he was the last to leave the bar. He was not pressed to leave. It seemed to him that the bar staff in their white shirts and black trousers could tell a man who could handle his liquor and who was lost in his own thoughts. They allowed him a wide berth and they swept the carpet and put upholstered stainless steel stools on the tables. They knew that he would leave eventually. Sussock drained his glass and turned and nodded to a young man wiping ashtrays, who nodded back and smiled. 'Good night, sir. Thank you.'

He walked to her flat. The flat with 'Williams' on the door. As he climbed her stair he recalled his own childhood vividly; he had grown up in a flat similar to hers. Except that he was one of six children in a room and kitchen and not in Shawlands but in the Gorbals, the old Gorbals of global infamy, and he remembered the screams in the night, the blood on the stair in the morning, and the toilet shared with three other families.

He knocked on her door. She didn't answer. He knocked again. He bent down and peered through the letter-box. No lights. She wasn't at home. He sank to the stone floor of the landing and leaned his head against the door.

CHAPTER 6

Saturday, 10.00–14.30 hours

Daniel Galley stroked the plaster cast of the skull and pondered Donoghue's question. He raised his eyebrows, pursed his lips and said, 'All day, I should think.'

'Quicker than I had anticipated.' Donoghue glanced out of the window at the university buildings, the neatly tended lawns, the trees evidently older than the buildings and obviously sensitively preserved and built around.

'Well, it's only the third that I've done.' Galley held the skull, Hamlet-like. 'It's still a new technique and the end result is a little like a Photofit in that I can only produce a likely approximation of what I believe that she looked like in life. The lips and nose, for example, have a shape or a characteristic which has no bone structure, not "betrayed" as we say, by the skull. So I have to guess and go by as much as you and the pathologist can tell me.' Galley placed the plaster cast delicately on the bench and picked up the report and read from it selectively. 'So . . . we know that it's a female skull, the forensic odontologist has given the age of the teeth as twenty years, plus or minus two years . . . all right . . . and you are assuming a white European, or Caucasian, female?'

'Yes.' Donoghue stood sideways on to Galley whom he

found to be a small man, balding, slight of frame, round spectacles and who moved stiffly in a starched white coat. Galley was a medical artist by profession. His studio at the university was decorated with delicate paintings in pastel shades of layers of muscle, of bone structures, of major organs. 'Yes,' he said again, 'we are indeed assuming a white European female on the basis that all missing person reports for the time of her disappearance are for Caucasians.'

'How long ago did she disappear, Mr Donoghue?'

'Perhaps twenty-five years ago, sir. She was buried in a shallow grave in a Lanarkshire field. Her parents will have assumed her dead many years ago. If you could put a face on the skull, somebody might recognize it, or we could check it against photographs of the missing persons, and if a name is suggested we could check the dental records and perhaps confirm an identity. If we could do that it would amount to a huge stride forward in our investigation.'

'Well, yes, as I say, Mr Donoghue, one day is all I need because the technique itself is really very straightforward. It's a theory that has been possible for centuries because it depends only on the pattern of muscle tissue on the skeleton and the existence of that knowledge can be traced back to Hippocrates. What held it up was the time we had to wait for alginate to be developed, that's the moulding compound used to make the plaster cast of the skull. Conventional plaster casts are not sufficiently strong to stand the innumerable little holes that have to be drilled into them to hold the cocktail sticks. Also, they are not strong enough to stand up to the pressure of clay being moulded, kneaded, on.'

'Cocktail sticks?' Donoghue smiled.

'Cocktail sticks. We drill holes and key locations, about fifty in all, so that they protrude as measuring sticks. Then we simply build up the modelling clay to represent the thickness of muscle and skin at those places as they would be in life, allowing for the differences inherent in age, sex and race. So that if memory serves, a Caucasoid female of twenty years will have a muscle thickness of three point five millimetres over her forehead, and four point seven-five millimetres above the eyebrows.' He reached for the folder. 'I've got a chart here. Yes, four point seven-five millimetres for the eyebrows of a twenty-year-old Caucasoid female. It's five point five millimetres over the eyes, eight point five millimetres over the upper lip, ten millimetres over the lower lip, ten point five millimetres over the jaw, five point seven-five millimetres beneath the chin, and so on; precise measurements for all points of the skull, using the skull as the matrix, the framework to hang the flesh on. Skulls appear identical, but they are very slightly different from each other and those differences are accentuated by the flesh and muscle which cover them. I find it ironic: whether this girl was considered pretty or otherwise in life would come down to her bone structure varying from the norm by a millimetre or two, but that would be quite sufficient to make a whole world of difference to her quality of life. So unfair.'

'Indeed. And a simple process.'

'Very simple in essence.' Galley closed the folder and replaced it on the shelf. 'What is difficult is the necessity of being painstakingly slow, and accepting the need for single-minded concentration. This is a job for the jeweller or watchmaker with his eyeglass, it isn't a job for the baker who likes to laugh and joke with his mates while pummelling his dough.'

'Certainly seems not.' Donoghue was not unimpressed. It was, he had long realized, the nature of police work, particularly of criminal detection, that the team is multi-faceted; there's a place for the brawn, for the kicking in of doors, and there's a place for the mild-mannered Mr Galley quietly working away, utterly engrossed in a small room in an obscure building of the university. 'Well, all I can do is leave you to it, sir.'

'Appreciate it, Mr Donoghue. I don't like people looking over my shoulder. If you give me a call on the 'phone about five, bell me at five, as they say in newspeak, I'll be able to tell you when I've finished it, indeed if I haven't already done so by then.'

Donoghue smiled. 'Thank you for giving up your Saturday, sir.'

'Oh yes, I'd quite forgotten that it was Saturday. You know, when I get in this room all notion of date and time vanish. Oh, but I respond to the 'phone.'

'Five o'clock.'

'Should see me almost there. Allowing an hour for lunch.'

Montgomerie pondered the shiny eyes, eyes of transparent scheming. He pondered the silver whiskers, a huge red mouth inside which were a few yellow pegs going up or down. He winced at the occasional blast of searing breath. Montgomerie shifted his position on his chair and glanced sideways, two youths sat on the scarlet horsehair bench at the far side of the bar, the track marks in their arms were visible to Montgomerie, even at that distance. One of the youths lolled his head about as if in a state of semi-consciousness, the other was completely catatonic. At intervals around the bench were places where the upholstery had been slashed and the horsehair pulled out in clumps. High on the wall, mounted on a metal shelf, was a television which had both the colour and the volume turned up too loud, beaming in racing from Cheltenham; images from another world. Montgomerie attempted to push his chair further back from the heat of the breath of the man with the whiskers and yellow teeth, but the chain which held the chair to the floor allowed him little leeway. Montgomerie was in the Gay Gordon, was sitting opposite Tuesday Noon, and he said, 'Come on, Tuesday, don't crap me around. I haven't had breakfast.'

Montgomerie had enjoyed a quiet night shift. A murder, routine, normal and grubby and cheap. One ned impales another on a five-inch thin-bladed kitchen knife, that being Scotland's number one murder weapon, and was still standing shaking and sobbing over the body of his 'mate' when the police arrived and gently took the murder weapon from his hands. There was a mugging, again, two burglaries, but it was Friday cum Saturday night in Glasgow, it was a uniformed cops night when alcohol and gangs of rival youths mix and when the cells fill slowly and steadily until they are full at around midnight. By 04.30 things had quietened and Montgomerie had turned his attention to the *Herald* crossword and managed all but two clues. Finally, awash with coffee, he pushed his chair back and put his feet on his desk. He did not attempt to sleep, but, subtly different, he gave up the attempt to stay awake and he entered a strange half-sleep, with eyes closed, brain dulled, but still heard noises inside the building, the banging of doors, the ringing of a distant 'phone, and occasionally noises from outside, the high-pitched hum of an early bus, the klaxons of fire engines, most probably, he thought, on an exercise. At 08.00 he became aware of an increase in the activity both inside and outside the building and as if helped by a built-in alarm clock he stirred, shook sleep from his eyes, washed in the toilets, straightened his tie and read over the cases he was to hand over to the CID day shift.

'Go and talk to your snout.' Donoghue reclined in his chair. It was 08.45, it had taken him fifteen minutes to wade through the cases that Montgomerie had handed to him and a split second to decide that there was nothing, nothing at all that warranted one minute of CID time to be diverted from the two main inquiries; the two inquiries that had caused him to come in to work on a Saturday. 'Go and talk to him, Montgomerie, he's been a good source of information in the past. I know the two incidents are unlikely to have been committed by members of the criminal fraternity, but we can leave no stone unturned. Your snout is a stone and I'd like him turned over.'

'Yes, sir.' Montgomerie's eyes felt tired.

Donoghue saw the look of weariness in the young officer's eyes, saw it and ignored it. 'So go and find him, we have a missing child, we have a lunatic who's been murdering women for twenty-five years. Like I said, Tuesday Noon is not likely to have any information but we can't afford not to turn him over. Hand these files to Abernethy, tell him to file them under pending.'

Abernethy sat at his desk in the CID room, young, fresh-faced, keen as mustard but with a veteran's look in his eyes. He saw Montgomerie advance on him with a pile of files. 'Work?' he said.

'Not yet.' Montgomerie stood in front of Abernethy's desk. 'This stuff was generated last night. Fabian says I have to hand it to you with the request that you file them under pending.' Abernethy took them and tossed them into a red wire basket on his desk. 'Somebody rattle your cage?'

'Oh, I wouldn't say that.' Montgomerie crossed the room with long, effortless strides. 'I mean, I've just done a full shift and I want to go home. I want to sleep, it's alien to the human condition that you have to prevent yourself from sleeping at night; now you can't sleep during the day either.'

'No?'

'No.' Said with controlled anger. 'No. In fact, no. I have to go to a bar up the Round Toll and talk to a smelly old guy who won't know a damn thing because the slave-driver wants to turn over stones, as he puts it.'

'Well, you cultivated him, your grass, I mean.' Abernethy leafed over a page in the file that he was reading. 'All you can do is go and do it. Then once you've done it, you can go home and collapse into your pit.'

'Aye.' Montgomerie sat on his desk. 'And maybe he won't be there anyway. I'm not hanging around if he's not there, that's for sure. There is a limit to how much I can and will be put upon, murder inquiry or not.'

'And missing child,' said Abernethy from behind the file.

'I'd be obliged if you didn't play games with my conscience.' Montgomerie swivelled round and picked up the 'phone, dialled a nine for an outside line and then a local number. 'Hi . . . it's me . . . sorry . . . do you want me to 'phone back . . . thought that we could do something tonight . . . no. I'm at work . . . I've got to work on a bit, have to go and see someone, can't say I'm looking forward to it . . . All right. Sorry I disturbed you. I'll 'phone you later.' He put the 'phone down, but only after she had slammed it down.

'You tend to forget people like to sleep in on Saturday mornings,' he said to Abernethy's file. 'I mean, when you work shifts long enough you forget that the rest of the world doesn't.' He looked at the telephone. 'I've just stirred up a hornet's nest.'

'Hope your snout makes it worth your while,' Abernethy grunted. 'Better go and dig him up. He'll be wanting his breakfast.'

'Aye.' Montgomerie stood. 'Take an hour to get there. It'll wake me up.' He slung his jacket over his shoulder and walked out of the room, along the CID corridor, down the stairs, signed out and walked out and into the Saturday morning bustle, sun shining off the red sandstone tenements and the grey of the concrete where the M8 cut a trench through the heart of the city. He walked up to the Round Toll, to a pub on a corner, which was once on the corner of rambling tenements, and which now stood alone, surrounded by coarse grass. Beyond the grass was a squat prefabricated Health Centre and beyond that, striding across the skyline, a massive housing scheme glistening in the sun. Beyond that, and behind, three yellow high rises, with a blue, blue sky and wisp of white cloud as the backdrop to it all.

Montgomerie pushed open the door of the Gay Gordon. It was 11.10. The bar had been open for a full ten minutes and would remain open for the next twelve hours, maybe longer if the landlord felt like chancing his arm by taking the risk that the police would be too busy to enforce the licensing laws. The publican glared at Montgomerie as he entered, he recognized a cop when he saw one, and by his glare he let Montgomerie know that he didn't like cops, not in his sawdust. Montgomerie ignored the glare; in fact, he found himself reassured by it. If ever, he thought, if ever the landlord of the Gay Gordon came to like him, then he would be worried about himself. Very worried indeed. He clocked Tuesday Noon in the corner, hunched over a whisky. Beyond him were two smackheads, above the spaced out smackheads was the television which showed pictures of horses bounding across a green sward. The sun streamed into the Gay Gordon through huge stained glass windows and served to create a soporific atmosphere, a hot-house effect, encouraging punters to stay in and drink, to stay in and avoid the reality of the world outside, the hard pavement, the fresher air, the stagger home.

Montgomerie strode up to the gantry and said, 'Whisky and an orange juice.'

'Orange juice.' Echoed with contempt. The barman glared at Montgomerie. Montgomerie held the glare. The barman moved in sudden jerky movements and slammed the glasses down hard on the richly polished hardwood gantry. Montgomerie dropped a five-pound note beside the drinks. The barman snatched it up, rang up the till and replaced it with smash. Montgomerie scooped up the coins, made a point of checking the change and then nodded icily to the barman. He walked across the sawdust through the sunbeams and sat opposite Tuesday Noon.

'We have a wee problem, Tuesday.'

Tuesday Noon's stubby fingers curled round the whisky and lifted it to his lips. He drained his glass in one go. Neat. He put it back on the table and breathed searing breath into Montgomerie's face.

'So we need all the help we can get, we're talking missing children, we're talking murdered women, maybe a week after they were abducted.'

Tuesday Noon looked blankly at Montgomerie and pushed the empty glass across the sticky surface of the table.

'Come on, Tuesday, don't crap me around. I haven't had any breakfast.'

'I don't hear nothing, Mr Montgomerie.'

'Didn't think that you would, Tuesday. It's most probable that neither the murder nor the abduction—if the little boy was abducted—was committed by a member of the crim. frat. But my boss says I've got to heave over stones. So I'm heaving over stones.'

'So I'm a stone now?'

'Among other things, Tuesday, among other things.'

'I'll keep my ears open, Mr Montgomerie.'

'Do so, Tuesday.' Montgomerie pushed the orange towards Tuesday Noon. 'Here, drink it. You can't have had any vitamin C since you last came of out Barlinnie: you know, that's the place where you get your vitamins by way of injection in your backside.'

'I ken.'

'See, Tuesday, a child's toy fits in. I don't know where it fits in but it fits in. A cuddly toy. A rabbit.'

'A rabbit.' Tuesday Noon smiled. It was one of the few times Montgomerie had seen him smile.

'A blue one.' Montgomerie looked at Tuesday Noon with an expression of serious intent. He wasn't going to let flippancy creep in. 'Look, Tuesday, I'm as serious as a heart attack. The furry toy fits in with the girl's murder. We don't know much about the missing child, the missing boy, we have nothing to go on there. Help us with either, Tuesday, and we'll continue to forget about all those outstanding warrants and we might even let you have Friday afternoon off. This is serious, Tuesday. Heavy Duty.'

Tuesday Noon pushed the empty whisky glass closer to Montgomerie.

Montgomerie stood. 'Counting on you, Tuesday.'

It was the explosion inside his head that woke Sussock. Or so it seemed. It may equally have been that he awoke to an endlessly exploding brain. He groaned and opened his eyes and looked across a green expanse towards an off-white cliff topped with a lip of silver. Just to one side of him was a tall thin black stem. He shut his eyes and the explosion subsided and was replaced by an intense pain which ran round the front of his forehead. He let out a second, longer, louder groan and opened his eyes once again. He took stock of his position. He was clothed. There was a pillow under his head and a blanket had been draped over him.

He was lying underneath Elka Willems's kitchen table.

He levered himself up and sat at the table and in a well-practised manœuvre he placed his right hand to his head, his thumb above his ear, the fingers of the right hand to the centre of his forehead. It was, he had once been shown, and subsequently had always found, a near-mystical way of making the pain of a hangover disappear. It was also a lot safer and healthier than painkillers. Sussock laboured under a Calvinistic streak in that he had brought this upon himself, he believed, therefore he had to endure it until it ran its course. Painkillers were in consequence forbidden, but magical use of finger and thumb on cranial pressure points was permitted. Using his left hand, he filled the kettle and made himself a mug of coffee from the jar of instant and the mug of milk obviously and thoughtfully left beside the clean mug by Elka Willems for him.

Carrying the coffee back to the table, he saw the note left for him by Elka Willems propped prominently up against the bottle of HP Sauce. In a round generous hand she told him how she had knocked up a neighbour to help her drag him into her flat. As he read the note Sussock uncurled his long bony fingers from the mug and put his left hand up to his head, to join his right and shut his eyes. It was another incident to be filed away in the recesses of his mind, which like so many other similar incidents would leap suddenly to the forefront of his mind, and do so when least expected, and would continue to do so, so long as he retained his mental faculties. In this way he was haunted by endless sins of social ineptitude which stemmed back to his teenage years. Elka Willems's note continued, inviting him to help himself to coffee and food. The hot water had been left on if he wanted to shower, but whether he showered or not could he please turn it off before he left the flat. There was a change of clothing in 'your drawer'. She had gone on to explain that she didn't know if he had any plans for the day but Fabian had all but cancelled leave and was coming in himself that day.

Oh, Saturday. Sussock suddenly realized that it was Saturday. He had a free weekend once every six weeks, and this was his free weekend. He glanced at the clock on the wall, a white face, Roman numerals within a pine frame. It was midday. He'd go in. He'd shower off, eat something, drink more coffee, change into clean clothing and go in. It was her way of telling him to do so, to score a point in his own favour.

*

'It's the not knowing.' The man spoke as much to himself as to the women who were also present in the room. He was tall, bespectacled, bearded, balding. 'You hope for the best, you can only hope for the best, and you try to shut the worst out of your mind but it's not so easy. It's always the worst that floods into your mind.'

The man's wife sat beside him and she reached out her hand for his. Elka Willems knew that she was barely preventing herself from bursting into floods of tears.

'You keep reproaching yourself.' The man squeezed his wife's hand as he talked it out of himself. 'You ask yourself if there was anything that you could have done, anything that you could have done but didn't. We warned him strongly about strange men.'

'I keep going up to his room.' Edwina Moore breathed deeply. 'Stupid, I know, but I do it, I just want to put my head round the door to see if he's sneaked back into the house and gone up to his room. Each time I open the door I think this time, this time, just let him be there to turn round and smile at me as I knock and enter, and each time I build up a little hope and each time there is a little disappointment.'

'Came back from North America yesterday,' said the man. 'Cut the lecture tour short, it was no big deal in the circumstances, the Yanks were full of concern, they're really into the concept of family in a big way. Couldn't have been more helpful and more pleasant about it. Haven't slept properly, it's Saturday today?'

Elka Willems nodded. She had been in the house for perhaps fifteen minutes, had stepped into the hallway and had circumvented unpacked suitcases and a baseball bat still with the price tag on the handle, and had upon invitation turned into the cool of the Moores' north-facing living-room. She had taken a seat and was again pleased to see books on the bookshelves. It had become her recent and frequent experience that in many homes bookshelf space had been given over to pre-recorded videos usually with titles like *Exterminator 27*. It was, it seemed to her, the way of things in late twentieth-century Glasgow. But the Moores were academics, they had use, need, and respect for books. Elka Willems had relaxed easily in the room, she found the books warm and softening.

'That's quite understandable,' she said, leaning forward in a concerned manner. She could only imagine the endless torture of having a child abducted or go missing for a period now measured in days. 'We are doing all we can, we've searched the areas in the locality where he is most likely to be, we've used dogs to do that, far more efficient than humans.'

'So I understand.'

'We've done house-to-house, it's rather a pity that it's not term-time, we can reach more children that way. Reach them for more information, reach them to warn them.'

'Of course . . .' Edwina Moore nodded. She wore loose-fitting clothes and had tangled hair. Elka Willems thought that she could look very fetching if dressed, but the woman clearly had a bohemian contempt for superficial appearances, so common, Elka Willems had found, in families similar to the Moores: brainy and bookish. She also had had, it appeared, her son, her only child abducted. Pride in appearance was not going to be high on her list of priorities. 'It never occurred to me that another child had been snatched.'

'One hasn't,' Elka Willems quickly reassured her. 'But it's a possibility that we must bear in mind. Another possibility is that he may be being held for ransom. I suppose you would have told us if you had received a ransom demand?'

'Yes.' Edwina Moore spoke with a solemn finality. 'And if we receive such a demand you will be the first to know.'

'Thank you.' Elka Willems stood. 'And for our part, we will of course let you know as soon as we have any news at all. Pleasant or otherwise.'

'We appreciate it.' Edwina Moore forced a smile.

Elka Willems said she'd see herself out.

Daniel Galley picked up a damp cloth and wiped the brow of the head which he was painstakingly building up. He was slowly, layer by layer, building up the modelling clay to the top of the pegs he had inserted at strategic places into the alginate base. Already the face was human and female, a little Neanderthal at the moment and still lacking hair, but with his skilled, experienced eye Galley could tell that the young woman who had been buried in a Lanark-shire field some twenty-five years earlier would, when he had finished, reveal herself to have been attractive; very attractive indeed. He glanced at his watch, 12.30, and then out of the window: a pleasant day. He had come to the end of a phase in the reconstruction of the face, a natural break in the process. Time for lunch, time for a stroll to Byres Road, and a meal in the vegetarian restaurant in the arcade. That would be good. He peeled off his smock and hung it neatly on the peg on the door. He slid into his light summer jacket and thought with pleasant anticipation of the vege-tarian restaurant in the arcade.

'Bought them from the cash and carry,' said the man, smart in a jacket of a loud checkered pattern, pushy careerist, self-serving, as well as being far too young to be the manager of a city centre toy shop. Or so thought Abernethy.

And for his part, Troy Floyd thought that the gawky, awkward, nervous man, ludicrously holding a huge toy rab-bit, was too young to be a cop and he had insisted on scrutinizing Abernethy's ID before turning his attention to the rabbit. 'We still have a few left.' Floyd wondered if Abernethy knew how ridiculous he looked walking along Argyle Street on a Saturday, holding a big furry rabbit. 'They were fashionable,' he added, 'and competitive, many shops sold them, Mr Abernethy, they were the flavour of the month a month or two ago. That's how the retail trade works with respect to toys, a few steady sellers, the hardy perennials as you might say, train sets for the boys and dolls for the girls, and then along comes something that grabs the mass fascination of childhood, their collective fascination if you like, like the rabbits which were a minor success, went like snow off a dyke for a few weeks and then stopped selling. You look disappointed,' said Troy Floyd with a smile and Listerine-laden breath.

'I am,' Abernethy replied coldly. 'Strange, but I was hoping that you could identify the person who bought this particular toy, provide name and address and everything. We'd like to speak to him.'

Troy Floyd smiled and shrugged his shoulders.

'Who is the wholesaler?'

'Sihan Brothers.'

'Where are they?'

'Over the bridge and turn right, Kingston-upon-Clyde. Where else would you find wholesalers in Glasgow?'

'All gone now, sir,' said Ali Sihan. 'I'll inquire of my brothers but they are now discontinued from Hong Kong.'

'Your brothers?'

'The rabbits, sir, the rabbits were sold, many, many thousands of them from many different retailers.'

'Many different retailers,' echoed Abernethy, rapidly coming to terms with a cul-de-sac.

'Large and small, sir.'

'Large and small.'

'Would you like a plastic bag with which to carry away your rabbit, sir?'

It was Saturday, 13.10 hours.

Saturday, 13.10 hours

Fabian Donoghue sat at his desk. He had taken off his jacket and had sat back in his chair reading the handwritten submission on the child abduction/disappearance and the double murder, prior to the reports being sent for typing. In his free hand he toyed with the lens, apparently from a pair of spectacles, which was wrapped in a self-sealing Cellophane sachet and which had been sent up by Elliot Bothwell in accompaniment with his report.

Donoghue had left his home in Edinburgh at nine that morning amid deeply felt but muted protest from his wife and somewhat louder protests from his children at his having, once again, to work on Saturdays. He had kept his voice calm and his manner firm, quite simply insisting that he was going: end of story. In his car on the mid-morning weekend empty motorway he was not at all concerned about the protests his family had made: their voices rang not in his ears. He slipped the Rover into overdrive and settled back to enjoy the ride as the car took him to Glasgow at a modest sixty miles an hour with the engine doing little more than idling. He thought that there was a young boy somewhere, maybe dead, maybe captive, who wasn't able to protest. In the coming years Donoghue envisaged political discussions with his grown children and he would doubtless be arguing along the lines of: 'Well may you protest, but at least you *can* protest!' In a similar way, his wife turning her back on him and sighing and reaching for a coffee-stained mug to wash did not concern him. There were two women who died when they were young, whose bodies had been taken from shallow graves in stony Lanarkshire fields, who would never have a husband or a family. But Mrs Fabian Donoghue, like her children, could at least complain.

He had reached P Division at Charing Cross at 10.00 a.m. and had sat at his desk, filled and lit his pipe, had begun to read the handwritten submissions and he had also sat back and pondered. Once that morning he had risen from his desk and walked across the carpet and stood looking out of his window at the square and angular buildings on either side of Sauchiehall Street. Somewhere, he thought, somewhere out there was a man abducting women, holding them captive for up to a week before drowning them in a bath of saline solution. After which he drove the corpses to Lanarkshire and buried them in a shallow grave . . . or driving them to Lanarkshire and then drowning them and burying them local to the locus of the murder. And also, somewhere out there among the weekend humanity T-shirted and sun-creamed, was a man or a woman or both who had abducted a child, or who had abducted and murdered a child and had hidden his still to be discovered body; or else the man or woman or both did not exist at all and Tim Moore's decomposing body would rise, grotesque, to the surface when the first rains of autumn flushed the reedbeds in the Forth and Clyde canal.

He felt the sunlight burn his face and stepped back into the shade and pipe-smoker's fog, and was amused that he feared the harm the depleted ozone layer might allow the sun to do to his skin yet was blissfully dismissive of the damage the Dutch tobacco with the twist of dark shag was doing to his heart and lungs and throat and blood pressure.

A little after midday he left the office for some lunch and took a short stroll to clear his head. At 13.30 he was back at his desk, body and mind refreshed, re-reading the submissions and toying with the lens encased in Cellophane.

There was a reverent tap on his door. Donoghue paused

and then said crisply. 'Come in.' Only then did he look up.

Abernethy stood in the doorway. He looked nervous and exhausted, as though he had been undertaking hard physical labour under a hot sun. He held a plastic bag in one hand.

'Yes, Abernethy. Come in.'

Abernethy approached Donoghue's desk. 'Drawn a blank on the rabbit, I'm afraid, sir.' He held up the plastic bag and lowered it again.

'Didn't think we'd get anywhere with it. But it was worth a try.' Donoghue took his pipe and pointed to a vacant chair in front of the desk. 'Leave it there, please. Have you had your lunch?'

'Not yet, sir.

'Well, grab something and then take this along to the Eye Infirmary.' Donoghue put the lens on the edge of his desk. 'See an eye specialist, or an optician, anyone who can tell you something about that lens.'

'Very good, sir,' Abernethy stammered. 'In fact I'm not so hungry. I don't eat much during the day in the summer. I'll get right on to it now.'

'Good man.' Donoghue returned his attention to Bothwell's report.

Abernethy turned and left Donoghue's office and then Donoghue heard him grunt and say, 'Sorry, Sarge.' Donoghue looked up to see Abernethy and Sussock sorry-sorry their way past each other in the doorway of his office.

'Ray.' Donoghue beamed as the elderly detective-sergeant entered his office. Donoghue thought he looked frail.

'Sir.' Sussock closed Donoghue's door and sank into one of the vacant chairs without waiting to be invited: it was a privilege of age and a working relationship of mutual respect.

'It's your free weekend, Ray. You know you are not supposed to be working.'

Sussock squeezed his eyes. 'Aye.'

'I mention it only, Ray, because it is not unknown for officers, and people in other walks of life as well, to go on the batter and get themselves up for work the next morning, and go in. It's as though an automatic pilot sets in . . . they forget it's their day off . . .'

'It shows?'

'It shows.' Donoghue nodded. 'The bloodshot eyes, the breath overladen with coffee and strong mints . . .' He reached for the 'phone on his desk and dialled a two-figure internal number. 'Hello, Donoghue . . . I'd like a pot of coffee and two cups in my room . . .' 'Yes, sir, now, sir.' He replaced the 'phone. 'So what brings you in if not your automatic pilot?'

'I heard the jungle drums, sir, they spoke long and they spoke forceful, and they spoke of major inquiries, of all hands to the pump, of the possibility of leave being cancelled . . .'

'Good man, I can certainly use you. I'll sort out a couple of days in lieu . . . Lord knows when.'

Sussock shrugged. 'What's the state of play, sir?'

'Pretty well static, I'm afraid. We're still turning over stones, no definite line of inquiry in either case. We'll get a lead in time, of that I'm certain, in one inquiry or the other. No leads on the little boy, the house-to-house in Broomhill and Jordanhill areas hasn't turned anything up, but often a house-to-house will prompt a delayed reaction.'

'I didn't remember when the officer called, but the next day I suddenly remembered . . .'

'Exactly, Ray, exactly. We can still hope for that response.' Donoghue lit his pipe. 'So he's either been abducted or he hasn't. If he has, he's either still alive or he isn't. If he hasn't been abducted he's dead.'

Sussock took his hand from his eyes.

'Dead, Ray. After this time he's dead. Either murder or fatal accident, body still to be discovered.'

Sussock nodded with a certain air of resignation. 'So we hope that he's been abducted.'

'We hope he's been abducted.' Donoghue sucked and blew on his pipe. 'Of the double murder, we now have the identity of the first to be discovered and the most recent victim. Richard King has dug up a shady, shadowy world of alcohol abuse and part-time prostitution, quite the other side of the coin from a twee existence in Egypt. The second victim, rather the second to be found but the earlier by about twenty-five years—'

'The one whose grave I was standing guard over all those years ago when I thought I was standing guard over a stolen motor—'

'The very one. She hasn't as yet been identified, but her head and face is being reconstructed as we speak by a medical artist.'

'A what?'

'Sort of chap who constructs anatomical diagrams. He's practising a recently developed technique of building up the face from a cast of the skull. The skeleton and teeth will tell you the age, sex and ethnic group, the textbooks will tell you the appropriate thickness of the skin for any given part of the skull depending on age, sex and ethnic group.'

'Simple.'

'I made it sound more simple than it is. In essence it seems straightforward and I suppose it is, but the process is slow and painstaking, the measurements are measured in millimetres. A job for a professional and a job not to be hurried. Apparently the shape and size of the nose and the thickness and shape of the lips have to be guessed because those aspects of appearance are not determined by the shape of the skull, but a reasonable speculation is used to get a result which is, I'm told, strikingly similar to the real thing. That's being done right now—'

A tap on his door.

'Come in.'

A WPC in a starched white shirt entered carrying a tray on which was a tall coffee pot and cups and milk and sugar.

'Thanks,' said Donoghue, 'just leave it on my desk, please.' He waited until the WPC withdrew before going on. 'Perhaps,' he continued when his office door clicked shut behind the WPC, 'perhaps that's something you could get on with. You're a bit too fragile to do any running around and interviewing.'

'I'd appreciate a quiet job, sir.' Sussock smiled. 'Can I pour your coffee?'

'Thanks. Just milk.'

Sussock grinned and said that he'd make his black.

'What to do, Ray, I would think, is get all the missing person files on young women from that period, about twenty-five years ago, those that are still open, of course, take the photographs out and when Mr Galley 'phones us from the University to say the model is complete—'

'Take the photographs up and see if one matches.'

'Right. If there is a match, ask the Dental Hospital for her dental records, get them over to the GRI. You might have to contact Dr Reynolds at home, ask him to check the records against the teeth in the skeleton in the mortuary. If they match, we've got a result.'

'Couldn't be simpler.' Sussock sipped his coffee. Delicately.

'Ray?'

'Sir?'

'You entice a girl back to your flat.'

'Yes, sir.'

'You murder her.'

'Most foully.' Sussock held his head.

'Well, drowning will do. Then you bury her.'

'In a field.'

'In a field. The question is, do you drive her to the field when she is alive or dead? I can't think what would make Sandra Shapiro be willingly driven from Glasgow to Lanarkshire unless she knew her murderer. We can, I think, discount that because if she did know him, we have to assume that the girl whose face is presently being reconstructed also knew the same man. Unlikely, I think, especially given the twenty-five-year gap between the events.'

'Also the rope marks to wrists and ankles suggests restraint.'

'Agreed. It would be difficult to transport a trussed-up and struggling girl all the way to Lanarkshire without attracting attention. If she was doped up, or boozed up in Sandra's case, she would be a dead weight and if so, he might as well carry a dead weight . . . Sorry, Ray, I'm shooting in the dark.'

'Why are you suggesting a city centre flat or some premises in the city, sir?'

'Because Sandra dabbled in prostitution. Once or twice a week she would work the street. I think she willingly entered the car of the man who was to murder her. I do not think she would have got in if he had said he was going to drive her out to Lanarkshire.'

'So he's got a gaff in the city?'

'I think so. Also because the location of the graves is too far apart to suggest local knowledge. They are in the same general area, that's all.'

'It would be more logical to murder her in the city and then drive the body to Lanarkshire in your own time.'

'I think I agree, I think the locus will prove to be in the city, but you know the thing that worries me, Ray, is that we are not dealing with a logical mind here. This person is not playing games with us, he's not leaving bodies where they'll be found, he's not sending us anonymous letters or tape-recordings, he hasn't got the brinkmanship quality so common among serial killers and which eventually brings their downfall.'

'One hopes.'

'Indeed.' Donoghue sipped his coffee. 'No, this bloke, he just gets on with it, no attempt to gain attention. He abducts, and after one week's imprisonment, he murders and then buries the corpses in a field in a remote area, and he's been at it for twenty-five years at least. He drowned one in a saline solution, the other he covered with rocks taken from the shore. He steals cars to transport the bodies but leaves the car at the scene and walks away. There is no logic at all, not even an insane logic that would at least give us a handle on this guy. And you know what I think about the saline solution and the pebbles? I think nothing.'

'Nothing?'

'Nothing. I think we are going to waste an awful lot of man hours looking for a significance in them. They mean nothing except that the murderer is insane. They fall into the same category as his leaving the car at the burial scene. He might have a reason for doing so but they defy logical analysis and we leave it at that. Part of the skill of police work is learning to identify blind alleys. He's a weirdo. And these damn toy rabbits . . . Frightening.'

'How often have the police stood guard over stolen motors in Lanarkshire when in fact we've been guarding a corpse in a shallow grave?'

Donoghue nodded. 'How many more are there? And a man walking away from the car we stood guard over on Thursday afternoon.'

'Just two days ago, seems longer.'

'And he didn't bury her with his bare hands.'

'So, a man walking with a spade.'

'Or a spade found in the vicinity.' Donoghue put his cup down. 'A farm-to-farm, Ray. Let's go for it.'

'King can do it. He's on the back shift.'

Darkness. Darkness and these things that felt soft and furry. Rabbits, toy rabbits. And the woman, like a man, strong, muscular, quick movements, sudden movements and a bad smell, like she didn't wash.

His engine wasn't working any more. His daddy had told him that his body is an engine and you have to keep it going and you do that by putting fuel in. The fuel is food and drink. So drink when you thirst, eat when you hunger, because once the engine stops it's difficult to get it started again. The pain in your tummy means that you are hungry, but the pain can pass and when it's passed it's difficult to start eating again and that's when your engine stops working. His engine had stopped hours ago. Hours ago he craved for food, now if he was offered it he doubted if he could eat it. But the pain in his throat was real, it was still there, a bit of his engine was still working. The sides of his throat felt as though they were touching. He pressed his palms on the soft wallpaper and then licked them. There was a little moisture. He repeated the process.

Endlessly. It seemed endlessly.

'Would you mind spelling that, please, sir.' Abernethy smiled and held his pen poised.

'D-i-p-l-o-p-i-a,' the man in the white coat obliged. 'Diplopia.'

'And it means double vision.'

'That's it.' The man was young, textbooks on his desk. His office had a window which looked out from the Eye Infirmary on to peaked tenement roofs and then the cranes at the shipyard. 'You see, most often double vision is caused by external factors, a knock on the head or too much booze, in which case it's a question of getting the head injury sorted or allowing the alcohol to wear off. The double vision will then self-correct. Occasionally, and it's not common, though not rare, occasionally double vision is caused by a dysfunction of the muscles behind the eye, they're not acting in a coordinated manner and the result is Diplopia: double vision.'

'And this is a corrective lens?'

'Yes.' The young man held the lens in his fingertips. 'You see the distinct prism quality of it, a certain angularity if you like, rather than the smooth sheet of glass as in the normal lens like I am wearing.'

'I see it.' Abernethy nodded.

'This lens has no other purpose than to correct double vision.'

'Can you tell me anything else about the lens, sir?'

'Only the obvious. It's shape indicates that it has come from a woman's pair of spectacles, it's more stylish in its perimeter shape, the wearer is a woman.'

'A woman?'

'Well, yes, it's got a more elaborate shape. And it's an old lens. It's a glass lens. Lenses these days are made of plastic, half the weight, though somewhat thicker. Mind you, the Japanese are producing plastic lenses which are actually thinner than the corresponding glass lens would be. They're very, very sophisticated lenses. But I'd say this lens is about twenty years old. And it's well worn, scratched and battered with age. It's probably from an old discarded pair, but whatever, the owner of the spectacles from which this lens came would now be in her late middle years, I would say.'

Abernethy scribbled on his pad. 'Is there any way that the owner of this lens could be traced through optical records?'

'Not practically. For a lens of this age it would mean

trawling through the optical records for the last twenty-five years and it's not something that we could let the police do because only a fully trained optician could read the records. The manpower to do that doesn't exist, and even then there is no way of telling whether the records pertaining to this specific lens are at this hospital. This lens could have been obtained at any optician in—in Europe, at a hospital or from a private practice.'

'Thanks anyway.' Abernethy stood. 'You've pointed us in a direction anyway. We know that we are looking for a woman, a middle-aged woman. It narrows the field, but it's still a huge population to investigate.'

The eye specialist also stood and handed the lens back to Abernethy. 'You know,' he said, 'it's a bit of a long shot, but there's no harm in it. If that lens has recently been lost from a pair of spectacles and if those spectacles are the only pair that that lady has, which is unlikely because Diplopia sufferers are more likely than most spectacle wearers to have a spare pair, then she will shortly be presenting somewhere requesting a new pair of spectacles. Even if she has a spare pair, she'll be presenting because she'll need another spare pair of spectacles. So if you like, I'll alert reception to the possibility and ask them to contact the police if a lady with Diplopia presents herself requesting a new pair of spectacles. I'll also ask them to go back—how many days?'

'Oh, three days, sir.'

'Three days—to see if she already has presented. If she has only one pair she'll be walking about holding one hand over one eye, or she may have fashioned herself a patch for one eye. It's a stopgap cure for double vision, simply shut down one eye at any one time, keep alternating the eyes to keep them both working, but you can't live like that especially if you are a woman and more appearance-conscious than a man.'

'Thank you, sir. I'll do the same with the opticians in the city. I'll 'phone them tomorrow, work through the yellow pages.'

Abernethy 'phoned Donoghue from the pay-phone in the foyer in the Eye Infirmary.

Sitting opposite him, Sussock watched Donoghue scribble on his pad, the handset of the 'phone pressed between ear and shoulder. He said, 'Thank you, well done,' and replaced the receiver.

'It's a woman, Ray,' he said. 'The man who abducted and murdered two women and maybe more over a twenty-five-year period is a woman. 'That's the supposition at present but it's the best lead we've had. She's also thought to be middle-aged, which of course she'd have to be.'

'It's a lead, as you say, sir.' It was all Sussock could think of to say.

'And as Abernethy says, it narrows the field. But much more than that, because we are looking for a middle-aged woman who suffers from double vision. Not many of them about. At least the murder inquiry is beginning to crack open, Ray.'

There was a tap on his door. Sussock turned and Donoghue looked up. Elka Williams stood there. She seemed to Sussock to be both elated and shaken.

'Come in,' Donoghue invited.

'Sir, I've just had a 'phone call; I'll go out and follow it up, get a better description, but I think you should know this as soon as possible. It's about the little boy who has been abducted.'

'Tim Moore?'

'Yes, sir. Well, the 'phone call came from someone who lives in the same street: she 'phoned in response to the house-to-house we did.'

'Yes, yes.'

'Well, her son has just told her that a few days ago an

old woman drove up alongside him in a car and asked if he wanted to come with her to see some rabbits . . .'

Donoghue and Sussock looked at each other and from Elka Willems's vantage point in the doorway she clearly saw colour drain from Donoghue's face.

Donoghue was too stunned to speak. He groped for his pipe and lit it with clumsy agitated movements, movements which neither Sussock nor Willems had seen before; he did so as the implication of what Elka Willems had said sunk into his mind. Somewhere in this city, somewhere there was a monster in a human female form who was prowling the sunny parks and suburban streets and the red light district, and enticing young women and children into stolen cars, abducting them, holding them against their will and eventually drowning them in brine and burying them in shallow graves. She did it calmly and without show.

And she had been doing it for twenty-five years.

CHAPTER 7

Saturday, 17.00 hours

'It's certainly possible.' Daniel Galley held up the faded missing persons poster beside the recreated head. 'Yes, yes,' nodding slowly, 'we'll have a look at the others, draw up a short league but I think that this will be it.' He laid the poster down and picked up another and studied it. Eventually he shook his head and repeated the process with subsequent posters.

Galley had finished recreating the skull at 16.30 and being, he had often been told, a perfectionist, he added a little fine tuning to the nose and the lips, gave her a hairstyle that he thought suited, and finally satisfied, he left his workshop and waited in his office, picked up the 'phone and dialled the number DI Donoghue had given him earlier that day. 'It's ready,' he said, when he was put through to Donoghue.

Donoghue was sitting alone in his office still, hours after Abernethy and Willems had given him information within seconds of each other which had stunned him into the realization that the person who had abducted Tim Moore had also murdered Sandra Shapiro, when he took the call from Galley. Donoghue spoke briefly to Galley, thanked him and replaced the receiver. The call jolted him into action. He picked up the 'phone and dialled a two-figure internal number. 'Ray,' he said when his call was answered, 'can you get the missing person files from about twenty-five years ago, only the ones of young women, take the photographs or posters from the files and get to Mr Galley's office at the university, the Department of Medicine?'

'Yes, sir.'

'He's finished reconstructing the skull; hopefully one photograph or poster will match the head and face that he has created. If it doesn't, then we'll have to get a photographer up there to take photographs for a "Do you know this girl?" poster. But I'd like to avoid that if possible.'

'Very good, sir.'

'WPC Willems about?'

'She's following up the 'phone call, sir. Out getting a description.'

'Good, see that it's circulated to all the mobiles and uniforms, and that is I think as far as we can take it at the present. Try and get an early night, Ray. I think we'll be in for a long day tomorrow, long day Monday as well. I presume that you're coming in tomorrow?'

'If you wish.'

'You'd be more than welcome, Ray. More than welcome! In fact you can follow up the skull, if posters have to be made, if we luck out. If we luck in, you could still follow it up, you'll get access to dental records tomorrow when the dental hospital opens for a few hours for dental emergencies. It's a question of cross-checking the records with the actual teeth at the mortuary. Might have to disturb Dr Reynolds at home but that's the name of the game. I'll be in myself tomorrow, won't make me wildly popular at home but this case is beginning to crack, and there's a little boy imprisoned somewhere, every minute is critical. OK, Ray, let's go for it.'

Sussock went for it. He had a large file of neatly folded posters and unfolded photographs, each clipped inside a large sheet of protective paper. He carried the file under his arm as he walked from Charing Cross the short distance to the university, enjoying as he walked the handsome Victorian architecture basking in the sun as he felt only the solid sandstone city of Glasgow can bask, and glow becomingly in the early evenings of summer, and he enjoyed the rich foliage, and the blue and white above.

At the university, in the Department of Medicine, in Daniel Galley's office, he confronted the reconstructed skull. He would in normal circumstances have found it an unnerving experience. It was, though, particularly unnerving here: on a small pedestal, as if brought back to life, was the head of a girl appearing as she would have appeared at the moment of her death, and who had been buried in the ground a few feet behind the then Constable Sussock as he stood dutifully guarding a stolen motor vehicle in a Lanarkshire lane. At that time she had probably been dead for less than twelve hours, her family maybe wondering where on earth she could be. Now, in this room of constant humidity, he looked at the face of a head that he could have looked at twenty-five years ago if only he had had a countryman's eye and had been able to identify recently dug turf in a rough pasture. But he was a city cop and saw only a stolen car abandoned amid fields and trees and mountains in the distance; so unused to the country had he been that instead of walking up to the toy rabbit and picking it up, he had actually stalked it and had been so relieved that no one was there to see him do it.

'So who are you, little one?' Sussock spoke to the modelled clay as he laid the folder on Galley's workbench, 'What is your name, pretty one?'

'She is rather, isn't she?' said Galley, sensing Sussock beginning to drift into a world of his own. 'Or was. She was pretty. I mean, I've guessed at the lips and the nose. Thicker lips and a larger nose would have made her less pretty despite her bone structure. I may have been generous there, I gave her a lovely mouth and a neat nose, but I don't think I was. The nose and mouth are as they ought to have been given the overall thinness of the face. If her mouth or nose were any larger she was served a rough deal in life.'

'Well, let's see.' Sussock opened the folder.

'The reconstructed skulls are used like Photofits,' Galley said, to Sussock's ears somewhat defensively, 'in that they don't purport to be an exact likeness, just a suggestion of the likely appearance.'

'I see,' Sussock mumbled as he held up the first photo-graph and cast his eyes backwards and forwards between it and the head on the pedestal.

'You'll have to make allowances.'

'Uh-huh,' as Sussock held up the second photograph. He laid it down again and picked up a third photograph, this time a full missing persons poster and held it at arm's length.

He continued to hold it.

He handed it to Galley.

'Could be,' said Galley. 'Could very well be. The cheek-bones and chin and forehead look right. The lips are the same as I thought they might be, the nose is a little longer than I have made it.' He paused and considered the poster. 'It's certainly possible,' he said.

'We'll lay that one on one side,' Sussock said, reading the legend beneath the photograph. 'Could very well be that one, she went missing in June of that year; that's when I was chasing rabbits.'

'Sorry?'

'Nothing. It's just that we know that the girl whose face you have reconstructed probably disappeared in the summer months. It doesn't mean that we can discount the girls who might have disappeared in the winter months, but the summer is a good pointer. Let's press on. Three more to go.'

They pressed on. Quickly. Rapidly. And dismissed all three.

Sussock picked up the missing persons poster, the one he had put on one side. 'So, here you are, Mary Manning, after all these years. Nineteen years old on the day you died.'

'She'd have been a woman in her mid-forties now,' said Galley, a little unnecessarily thought Sussock, who did not yet feel brain dead, and was still well able to do his sums. 'At least her family will know.' Galley took off his smock. 'Late in the day but better than never knowing.'

'We won't know it's her for certain for a wee while yet,' Sussock told him. 'We'll have to check the dental records. Can't do that until tomorrow. Thanks for your help, sir.'

'Pleased to be of assistance.' Galley slung his smock over the back of a chair. 'I'll rescue what's left of Saturday.'

Sussock returned to P Division at Charing Cross. Yes, it was Saturday wasn't it?

*

It could be eye-shadow. It could equally be a fading bruise. King thought probably the latter because the other eye was not marked.

And because the woman looked timid. She reported that she had told the other officer. 'The older gentleman, sir, I told him I'd seen nothing.'

'Is your husband in?'

'Sleeping, sir. He came home with a good drink in him. Best not to wake him.' She spoke in hushed tones.

'I see.'

'But no, I didn't see anything, the house is in a hollow as you can see, as you'll have noticed, but no, I didn't see anything.'

There was a low howl from deep within the house, as if from a mortally wounded animal.

The woman seemed embarrassed. 'That's my man. He's asleep, he does that in the drink, even when he's asleep.'

'If you should hear neighbours speak of anything . . .'

'I don't see neighbours, sir,' said Linda McWilliams. 'I go to the shops in Carluke once a week and that's it. Apart from that the only person I see is my man.'

'Thanks anyway,' said King and turned back from the door. It was shut softly behind him.

He drove to the next farm. It was larger than the McWilliams's. It was easily visible from the road, it was more like a country house with a farm attached than it was like a conventional working farm in Lanarkshire.

'Didn't see anything,' said the man, calm, assured, clean shirt, flat cap, outdoor complexion, healthy but not weather-beaten, no sense of struggle about him that King could detect. The man seemed to King to be making much more of a success of tenant farming than McWilliams appeared to be making; or perhaps, King wondered, was this gentleman a successful and fortunate owner of his land?

'I've heard about it, of course, heard the scuttlebutt, also heard about the other body that was exhumed yesterday. The name's Farmer, by the way,' said with a flash of white teeth. 'Mr Farmer the farmer.'

'Mr Farmer,' King repeated. 'We tried to keep the exhumation yesterday as much of a secret as we could.'

'Farming country, Mr King. Not a lot goes unnoticed. You may not see anybody, but rest assured there are eyes on you, from a distance maybe, but they are on you. Night time it may be different, somebody buried two bodies without being seen, but they most likely did that at night. Besides which, the scuttlebutt's rife. Hasn't been better gossip for years.'

King's eye was caught by the graceful flight of a swan close to trees by the river.

'The cygnets are doing well,' said Farmer the farmer, catching King's gaze. 'I'm keeping an eye on them, there are some bandits about; lads from the estate in Carluke, not proper country boys, but small town lads who come out and rampage around, but the swan and her cygnets are well hidden. They haven't found her yet. I chase them off, the lads, if they get too close. Saw a fox close to the cygnets early one morning, had my gun, not supposed to interfere with nature, but what the hell. Besides, a fox had been at my chickens. So tell me, the scuttlebutt says that one corpse was fresh and the other was a skeleton and that there are more buried. Is that so?'

'Scuttlebutt may have a point. Tell me, how long would a fresh dug grave be noticeable to a countryman?'

Farmer shrugged. 'In rough pasture, in the summer, away from road or track, only a matter of days, before it grassed over or the cattle trampled it.'

'Days,' echoed King.

'That's all the time that would be needed. But while I didn't see anything, I wonder would a roll of carpet interest you?'

'It might indeed,' said King. 'It might indeed.'

In the outhouse Farmer lifted up the carpet and unrolled it.

'Nothing in it or on it,' said Farmer. 'Found it by the side of the road; hadn't heard of the body in the McWilliams's pasture at the time I picked it up, it seemed a useful bit of padding for one of the sheds, you can always find a use for a bit of carpet.'

King lifted it up. 'Can we take it outside?'

Out in the yard, under the mid-afternoon sun, King examined the carpet, looking at it sideways with Farmer watching, square foot by square foot. Then he stopped, supported a portion of the carpet with one hand and with the finger of the other, plucked a long human hair from the fibre, but did not dislodge it completely.

'Well done,' said Farmer.

'It's a human hair.' King replaced the strand, letting it fall back on the fibre. 'That's all we can say at present, but it's long enough to be a female hair. I'll have the carpet down to the Forensic Science Lab.' King folded the carpet. 'I'm sorry, but you've lost your treasure trove. Can you show me where it was found?'

'I'll take my Land-Rover. If you'd like to follow me in your car.'

The roll of carpet proved to have been found by the side of the road, adjacent to an area of long grass. King pondered the location. To his right, the McWilliams farm. To his left, in the distance, the town of Carluke.

'He went thataway,' Farmer said, evidently, King thought, reading his mind.

King glanced towards Carluke, grey roofs lying between a fold of green hills. 'You reckon?'

'I reckon strange behaviour: carry a body out here that's wrapped in a carpet, bury it and then not only do you leave the car but you carry the carpet for more than quarter of a mile before you discard it.'

'As you say.' King wanted to give little away.

A Land-Rover drove past, hood down, windscreen flattened on the bonnet, the owner naked to the waist. He and Farmer nodded to each other. 'My neighbour,' said Farmer. 'Or rather, his son. A long way for a bloke to walk with a carpet for no good reason that I can see. Tell me, have you found the spade?'

'The spade?'

'The spade he used to dig the hole.'

King conceded that they had not.

'Has to be around somewhere.' Farmer raised his eyebrows. 'Unless he carried it all the way home with him, which would draw a lot of attention to himself. I mean, who carries a spade at dawn? He left the car, scuttlebutt says so, he walked a quarter of a mile carrying the carpet he'd wrapped the body in, he probably carried the spade about the same distance.'

'It's not beyond the bounds of possibility.'

'Well, do you want assistance or do you want to do it alone?'

'Do what alone?'

'Cut back all this long grass. I think there's a spade in there somewhere.'

King nodded. 'All right. If we don't find it on the first sweep we'll organize a proper search later.'

'You're the boss.' Farmer advanced on a small tree, a young plant but well beyond being a sapling, and snapped two sinewy branches at the roots. He took them in his hands, each about four foot long, and shredded the leaves from them. He tossed one over to King. 'Just swipe away,' he said, 'cut the grass back; if the stick breaks you know where to get another. If you go to the McWilliams's gate and start there, I'll go to my gate and work towards you.

If we meet half way without finding anything we'll have done all we can.'

'Public spirited of you,' said King. 'If you find it don't touch it, or anything else that looks out of place, suspicious, or foreign.'

'Foreign?'

'As in a foreign object, foreign to the locality.'

'Understood. You know, I should pay you for this, at least for doing the stretch that's on my land. McWilliams can look after his own.' Farmer put the branch over his shoulder and walked jauntily down the road. A man, thought King, very much at home in the country.

Sussock entered his reasoned belief that the identity of the deceased female whose skeleton had been exhumed and whose head and face had been constructed by Daniel Galley, who had then left his studio to rescue what was left of his Saturday, was one Mary Manning, nineteen years old when she died, and whose home address at that time, twenty-five years previously, had been in Rawyards, Airdrie. He lodged a request for the missing person file to be signed out to him, reference to Sandra Shapiro murder inquiry, and he returned the other files to the collator.

There was no other readily identifiable task for him to address. No loose end he could quickly and neatly tie. He went home, strolling home in the calm summer evening.

He loved this city.

Malcolm Montgomerie strolled along the pathway in the grounds of Gartnavel General Hospital. The heat of the day had subsided, the early evening was comfortably warm without being oppressive. In the distance near the railway line, a group of children played with a ball. He approached a wooden bench and succumbed to the desire to sit down.

There was a chunk missing from his life; it seemed a

weight pressing on his stomach, and yet he had also felt strangely enriched and ennobled by the affair. He felt also a sense of anger, but it was anger directed at himself. He felt that for the first time in his life he had failed to come up with the goods, or was it, he wondered, simply that he had found the ceiling in his sex life.

Theirs had been a short relationship, unique in his experience in that she seemed to have called the shots, she held the initiative from day one, from their first meal where she had pushed his glass of grappa towards him and said, 'Come on, drink up, if we're going to sleep together tonight.' She was a product of her background, educated at the most prestigious girls' school in England, where she had kept wicket in the cricket friendlies against Cirencester Agricultural College, and where she had double-somersaulted with pike in the school diving team. She had, he found, matured into a sexually confident young woman of grace and beauty, courage and integrity; and a slimness which belied physical strength.

Finally, in the vegetarian restaurant of pine tables and climbing plants she had said, 'We won't be sleeping together any more.' She held the pause. Long hair about her shoulders, a lilac scarf about her slender neck. She held his stare. 'The spark just isn't there, Malcolm. I still would like your friendship, but we won't be doing "it" any more.'

He had seen her into a taxi and forced the smile as they said farewell. He walked in the still city, a city in the lull when the Saturday shopping had been done and before the Saturday revelries began, and found himself, both enriched and self-reproachful, in the grounds of the hospital. He sat on a bench, the hum of the traffic on Great Western Road reached him from one direction, the excited cries of children with a ball from the other, and in front of him, across the car park, the concrete edifice of the hospital.

He drew a deep breath and stood and walked towards his future. The vision in front of him was pleasant, of lushness and foliage: of life, and the sun was setting behind him.

But hey, her name was Pippa Scott. Five foot five inches tall and she didn't miss and hit the wall.

The sun, too, was setting behind Richard King when he found the spade. He found it after laying the grass low on a hundred yard stretch of bank, he found it when, despite cooling evening breezes, sweat poured from his brow and soaked his shirt under his armpits. He wiped his brow and found himself reluctant to relinquish the branch which had served him so well. He hailed Farmer, who turned and began to walk towards him, joining King as King lifted the spade by the shaft, avoiding the handle or the blade which might, he thought, hide fingerprints.

'Brand new,' said Farmer as King turned the tool, the blue of the blade and the varnish on the handle glinting in the evening sun.

'Used recently,' King added, nudging the dirt on the blade with his knuckles.

'It will have been used to dig the grave.' Farmer spoke with quiet authority, 'For a start, it's too narrow for farm work, it's not a farmer's tool. Secondly, it's not purchased locally.'

'No?'

Farmer shook his head. 'The only place to buy tools in Carluke is Beer's, they retail top of the range stuff like Spear and Jackson. That spade is junk. You found it just here?'

'Just here.'

'You know, this doesn't make sense. First he wraps her in a carpet, drives her in a stolen car to this field, buries her in a grave dug with a newly purchased spade. Then he leaves the car; that's madness itself, did he never hear of a quick getaway? Then he walks towards Carluke, carrying the carpet and the spade, probably counting the stars as he walks, then gets tired of carrying the spade and the carpet so he tosses them into the long grass. He could have launched the spade into the river, you might never have found it. Talk about being off your head, this guy's in a world of his own. No attempt to cover his tracks. Frightening.'

King could only nod. But he thought: This guy's a woman, friend, and that to my mind makes it even more terrifying. And she began to see double at some point in the evening because one of the lenses popped out of her spectacles and she didn't find it because we did.

'I'd be obliged if you'd keep this to yourself, Mr Farmer.'

'Oh, of course.' But King sensed some rare scuttlebutt in the Dadas Bar, Carluke, that evening; in the next few hours, in fact. The sort of scuttlebutt that would keep the smiling Mr Farmer the farmer well plied with the bevvy.

'The spade wasn't bought locally.'

'No chance.'

'The car was "liberated" in Glasgow.'

'Was it?'

'Yes.' That information was harmless. King let Farmer have it. 'So the culprit, I would assume, would make his way back to Glasgow from here. How would he do that?'

'Bus or train,' said Farmer. 'But he'd use the train.'

'He would?' King raised his eyebrows in a manner nakedly borrowed from DI Donoghue when he requested information.

'For sure.'

A pause.

'Well,' said Farmer, 'this business had to be done at night. Just had to be. Things start early outdoors around here and nobody saw anything suspicious.'

'Go on.'

'The first train into Glasgow leaves before the first bus.'

'That's hardly a full argument.'

'Well, this was planned, the stolen car, the spade purchased for the objective of digging the grave, the carpet purchased with the object of wrapping the body in to conceal it. All three discarded when the deed was done. I'd say it was planned, oddball, mad as a hatter, harebrained as it might be, but it was planned. If he plans like that he also plans his escape. I reckon he would have checked the bus and rail timetables and gone for the first transport out.'

'I remain unconvinced, Mr Farmer.'

'The other advantage is that Carluke is an unmanned station.'

King caught his breath. This time Farmer had something.

'It's at the edge of the town, down a leafy cul-de-sac. The point is that if he took the bus he would have had to hang around at the bus station and he'd be clocked as a stranger, he'd have to speak to the driver to get his fare. But with the train he could have remained out of sight in some shrubs, waited until he hears the rails start to sing, then hop across the footbridge and on to the train. He'd pay on the train and the first question the guards asks is, "Which station did you get on at, Jim?" He could well be inside Glasgow before he was asked for his fare. Equally, he might be seen getting on at Carluke, but that would be bad luck. It's a chance I'd take if I were him.'

'You have a point there, sir.' King nodded. 'You'd have made a good cop.'

'I was. Held a senior rank to you.' Farmer grinned. 'I was with the Lothian and Borders, worked in Leith. Like Dodge City on a Saturday night. Inherited a ton of folding green from a relative I didn't know I had, took early retirement, very early, and sank the cash into my farm. Never looked back. Good evening.'

*

'More like a man than a woman,' said the girl with a small face, a hardened face, cold, used, abused, eyes, cheap clothes and track marks in her forearms. 'I'd like to get back to the street; you know this has been a quiet night so far, a slow night. I'm getting strung out. I have to make another thirty quid before I can get my fix and I don't like having to work after midnight.'

'Two hours yet,' said Abernethy.

'Less. Last time I was really strung out I bit through the flesh in my thumb. I still have a scar. Look.'

'Not now. So this woman . . . ?'

'Can I smoke?'

Abernethy pushed a round piece of tin foil which had once contained a meat pie across the table. The girl took a ten-pack of cheap nails from a plastic handbag, lit it with a disposable lighter. She drew the smoke in deeply.

'Just how old are you?' asked Abernethy.

'They all ask that question,' the girl said, smiling, 'and I tell you, they divide into two groups: half are relieved that I'm over sixteen, half are disappointed. But I'm old enough, I've got two children taken from me by the children's panel on advice of the social workers. Social workers have more troubles than their clients. Couple of my regulars are social workers, one of them works in the night duty team, I see him in the afternoons, the other's at a hospital, I think. But looking young is something I use. I make good money from men who like little girls.' She looked at Abernethy and jabbed the air with her smouldering nail. 'Now that *is* a social service.'

'Dare say it is. Maybe you could tell us about your clients sometime, the ones that like little girls.'

'Sometime. Maybe I'll meet you half way, I don't want to put myself out of work, but I'll tell you what: if one of them really acts out of order, like asks me if I can get a real little girl for him, I'll feed you his name or car registration. Deal?'

'Deal.'

'What's your name, anyway?'

'Abernethy.'

'Abernethy. I like you, Abernethy. I think it's rich you ask me about my age. I'd say that you're too young to be a cop. You've still got a couple of spots on your face. Anyway, you're more civil than most cops. So I like you. When I was a wee girl our family doctor was Dr Abernethy. He was a nice man and that name makes me feel all warm inside.'

'That right?'

'Aye.'

'Tell me about this woman. That's the reason you're in here talking to me. When you've told me all, then you can go back to the street.'

'Aye, well, Sandra, Sandra's a good kid.'

'Was.'

'Was. That's going to take some getting used to.'

'Maybe you could learn from it.'

The girl shot a glare at Abernethy. He held it.

'Well, you get into cars with strange men as well, don't you?'

She looked at the Police Mutual calendar, blue on orange wall-covering. She looked at the grey plaster ceiling. 'But she had a problem. With me it's junk. With Sandra it was the drink.'

'We know.'

'She was better off than me and the other smackheads. See, with her she could work one night and earn enough for a three-day bender, and pay her rent and buy her food. With me eight hours on the street pays for one fix of junk with enough left over to puncture myself with in the mornings. Then I need money for food and rent. And she can leave off drink easier than I can let go of smack.'

'That's open to dispute.'

'Aye, it's like a dose of 'flu, coming off heroin. I've heard that. It's always said by folk who aren't on it. I've seen people in cold turkey, it doesn't look like any 'flu bug to me. Then they say it's in your head, and that's rich too because the one part of you that is OK is your head, your stomach's getting turned inside out and your legs are being power drilled, but your head's OK.'

'The woman?'

'Aye. So this man, only it's not a man, rolls up in his little car. A black Ford. He looked daft in it. Him so big and the car so tiny. Anyway I went up to check him out, you know how it's done, you've got to get it right on the first impression. He winds the window down and I see it's a woman. She said she wanted a girl for her husband who was old and ill and on the way out, wanted a girl to lie alongside him—original—but not what you'd call an attractive proposition, any girl would really jack up the price for that. A dying man . . .' She shook her head. 'But I wasn't strung out enough to consider an old man.' She drew on the nail. 'She was right to target a smackhead for an off-beat request . . . a strung-out smackhead gets so desperate that they'll do anything, I mean anything.' The girl dogged the nail in the cheap tin ashtray. 'Anyway she pestered, really pushy, and she had this manner about her —I've come across it before, years ago, a weird guy, he sort of pulled you towards him. I remember feeling like a fish on a line being reeled in. I wanted to resist but I couldn't. She had the same soft voice, gentle manner, but a look in her eyes which fixed you, so you couldn't walk away, and like this guy years ago, the woman in a black car just wouldn't take no for an answer, she made me want to get in the car.'

'But you didn't?'

'No. See, this guy I mentioned, years ago, I gave in to

him, gave in to his—his magnetism and got in his car. He drove me out to the Campsies and beat me up, gave me a real doing and ripped off all my clothes and stole my money. I made it back to the road as naked as the day I was born, a car stopped for me, I was OK then. I was off the street for a year after that and then—' she shrugged—'the needle.'

'I see.'

'But after that I have always been wary of the soft voice, the persuader, and that look in the eyes and when I run into a personality like that I turn and run. It's the only way to break free, you have to tear the hook out of you. That's what it feels like, as soon as they start looking at you and start to talk to you, there's a hook working it's way in.'

'So you turned and ran?'

'Yes. I heard the car drive off. I saw it later. I saw Sandra getting in.'

'What night was that?'

'Maybe a week ago.'

'Can't you . . .'

'No.' She shook her head. 'I wish I could. The days just blend and merge, you know, I can't tell you what day of the week it was.'

'You sure it was the same car?'

'No. No, I'm not sure. I was too far away.'

'But it was identical?'

'Same colour, same type, same evening thirty minutes later, same street . . . Too much of a coincidence.'

Abernethy nodded. 'I think you're right. Let's go for a description.'

'Like I said. I thought she was a man.'

'Big?'

'Big. Big-boned, masculine, heavy features, strong face, short curly hair, even had some whiskers, a few white hairs growing from her chin. She had a man's sports jacket, only when I got close did I see a woman's chest, a tweed skirt and heavy stockings. She wasn't pretending to be a man. Had sort of womanly spectacles, not fancy, twee, ultra-feminine spectacles, heavy framed, but a woman's frame none the less.'

Abernethy wrote on his pad. 'You don't talk like most of the girls who walk the street, Zoë Padbury.'

'Oh?'

'You've got a softer voice, use words like you have had an education.'

'I did have.' Zoë Padbury shrugged. 'My father is something enormous in British Steel, Scottish Division. I went to a private school, my two brothers are doctors. My father has disowned my, but my mother still prays for me. Don't tell me the only thing that stands between me and recovering all that is a dose of 'flu. I don't want to hear it, not now.'

'OK. So this woman, looked like a man. What did she want?'

'I need to work, Abernethy.'

'Answer the questions. Then you can go.'

'She wanted a girl. She said she wanted her old man to have a girl.'

'Old man.'

'Her husband. She said he was sick, I thought she meant that he was on the way out, and she wanted to have a young thing to ease him in his final hours.' Zoë Padbury shuddered.

'I'm surprised someone agreed to that.'

'Who says anybody did?' Zoë Padbury replied, revealing to Abernethy quick wits behind the racked muscles and the piercing, aching joints of the addict shortly to be in need of a fix. 'That's what she said to me. She probably recognized me as a smackhead and knew a smackhead would do things other girls wouldn't. Maybe she asked Sandra something else. A woman once hired me for her son, you know, his first time, maybe it was something like that, or maybe she smelled her breath and invited her to a drinking party.'

'What was her voice like?'

'Husky. Slow. Deliberate. I think.'

'Think harder.'

'It's hard to remember. I turned her down almost immediately, the manner she had and her proposition made her strictly a no go area. Anyway, I'd just shot up, I could pick and choose for an hour or so. That's the way it is. If she'd have stopped me six hours later and the work had been slow I would have agreed. You don't know what it's like, Abernethy. Listen, if I needed a score badly enough I'd climb into bed with a scabby horse. Can I go now?'

'No.'

'No. Come on.'

'Oh.' Zoë Padbury put both arms across her stomach and shivered.

'We'd like you to help us make up a Photofit.'

'Couldn't miss her.' The guard stood on the open door of the carriage. 'Aye, I remember her well, held one hand over her eyes, the right, I think. I was on morning shift last week, last shift of the run before I came on to back shifts this week. That was the first train of the shift, that would put us into Carluke at about six-thirty. She came running over the footbridge and jumped aboard. Where did you know where to find me?' He glanced along the length of the low-level platform at Glasgow Central.

''Phoned the depot. Told them I wanted to speak to the guard on the first train out of Carluke on Thursday. They told me to wait for this train.'

'I see. Aye, a big old woman, but strong, she'd been digging, had that smell of the garden about her, you know the scent of freshly turned soil. Not to mention the dirt on her shoes.'

'The garden,' said King as the train doors whirred shut.

The explosion of light hurt his eyes long after the flash, long after the camera had been lowered, long after she had shut and locked the door again. The door had been thrown open, she stood there filling the door frame, like his father filled the door frame and she stood there, with a patch still over one eye like she had when she stopped her car that day and a camera in the other. He croaked that he was thirsty. She had raised the camera and popped the flash. Tomorrow, she had promised. Tomorrow, or the day after, all the water you can drink.

A whole tub full. Just for you, she had said. Then we'll go somewhere. Somewhere in the country,

CHAPTER 8

Monday, 09.00–Midday

Abernethy held the 'phone to his ear. It was the tenth call of the morning and already his ears burned as if from a childhood cuffing.

'DC Abernethy . . . no, Abernethy . . . yes, ask for me or the duty officer CID officer . . . duty CID officer . . . we're 'phoning all opticians in Glasgow . . . if an adult female patient contacts the optician, or has contacted the optician in the last few days, and who suffers from a condition apparently called Diplopia . . . d-i-p-l-o-p-i-a . . . double vision, and who may have lost or damaged her spectacles recently and wants a replacement pair . . . can you inform us immediately? Yes, it's vital. Urgent . . . well, yes, any patient with Diplopia if you like . . . thank you.' He replaced the 'phone and picked it up again. There were twelve columns of ophthalmic opticians in the Glasgow yellow pages.

'It's her all right.' Reynolds studied the dental charts and then looked at the teeth of the skeleton, by then fully rinsed with industrial alcohol. 'No doubt about it. You see the front incisors, how twisted they are. And the bridgework here? Sorry I wasn't at home yesterday, by the way.'

'Yes, sir,' said Sussock. But he didn't. To him it was just a rinsed down skeleton with gaping orbits and protruding teeth. When it was fleshed he had stood a few feet away from it enjoying a job he had thought 'a skive'.

'Well, the identification is positive. I have no objection to you having a forensic odontologist to come over and give a second opinion, but I am satisfied it's the skeleton of—' he looked at the top of the dental chart—'Mary Manning.' He replaced the cloth over the face of the skeleton and slid Mary Manning back into the bank of metal drawers.

Sussock left the GRI and walked out into the mid morning sun, already high, a blue sky and a welcome cooling breeze. He breathed deeply; soon, all too soon, he knew he would not be able to, soon, before he knew it, the thin air of autumn would attack his lungs. He had been a heavy smoker in his youth, smoking on duty when he could, as when, twenty-five years earlier, he had enjoyed a cigarette while standing guard over a stolen car, when all the while he was standing guard over the freshly buried corpse of Mary Manning whose skeletal remains he had just identified. It had been that summer, he recalled, that he had stopped smoking. The habit was doing his lungs and his pocket no good at all: in fact, it was doing both great harm. Then years later the chest pains started, they started in autumn and stayed until spring. 'You're a smoker,' said the GP. 'I was,' said Sussock, 'but I stopped, years ago.'

'Doesn't matter. You did it and it's caught you up.' Sussock had come to loathe and dread the winter: the advertisement for the sports car, 'Goes like a Scottish summer, grips like a Scottish winter,' held special significance for him. But hope was perhaps on his distant horizon, perhaps a divorce, perhaps retirement: soon he could spend deep midwinters snug and warm in a room and kitchen, or on a pensioner's holiday in Spain.

He reached his car, opened the door and let the windows down to allow the car to 'breathe'. Then he drove to Rawyards.

Rawyards, on the north-eastern fringe of Airdrie. Narrow streets, low-rise council housing scheme, on a hillside, few amenities. Not a pleasant place to live during the summer. In winter it was the end of the earth.

He went to Northburn Street, to No. 267, the last known address of Mary Manning. It was a flat in a block house, a building of four flats, two up and two down. The front garden was overgrown, a bin liner of domestic refuse had burst and its contents lay strewn on the grass, most probably by the dogs, thought Sussock. The pathway was pitted and broken. He went to the second door at the side of the house. It was scarred as by slashes with a knife, the glass pane had been sheeted over with plywood. Sussock knew what sort of house-hold was behind the door. He could even smell the sickly sweet aroma of alcohol before the door was opened. He rapped on the door and heard the sound echo in the hallway, no floor or wall covering to deaden it, the sound of his knock bounced clearly off floorboards and plaster walls.

'Who is it?' A woman's yell.

'Police.' Sussock spoke through the letter-box.

Sussock heard a heavy footfall come down the stairs. The door was opened. Sussock reeled from the alcohol fumes.

'Yes?' The woman stood at the bottom of the stairs, which, as Sussock had surmised, were uncarpeted. She was well built, dirty, matted hair, a round, reddened face ingrained with dirt. She wore a red T-shirt which revealed thick, flabby arms; a too small pair of jeans gave way to dirty bare feet. Sussock thought her to be about sixty but knew she could well be in her early forties. It's what Raw-yards and alcohol can do to a woman.

'Police,' said Sussock. He flashed his ID.

The woman looked at him with narrowing eyes.

'I'm looking for a Mrs Manning.'

'You've found her.'

'You have a daughter, Mary?' Sussock glanced over the woman's shoulder, bin liners and empty bottles sat on the stairway leading from the flat to the doorway. A man moved across the landing. He was stripped to the waist, he moved slowly, sluggishly, over-concentrating. He didn't notice the open door below him, or Sussock talking to Mrs Manning.

'My stepdaughter,' said the woman. 'Though she was just five years younger than me. See, me, I married her dad when she was eighteen and I was twenty-three.' She spoke with a searing hot breath, then added by means of expla-nation, 'We are on a wee bender.'

'Been going long?'

'Two days. We've got enough to see us through today, make it a good three-day bender.'

'Maybe I should come back when your head's clearer?'

'My head's fine,' the woman snorted.

Sussock nodded. He'd been this way before, Mrs Man-ning's information would probably be accurate but she would also have little or no recollection of giving it to him when she came out of the 'bender' in one day's time. 'So, Mary?' he said.

'She disappeared. Can't say I was sorry. Me and her just didn't get on. I heard she left to walk the streets in Glasgow. She left about a year after I moved in with her dad. Her dad died two years ago but I kept the house, had it put in my name.'

'Any other relatives?'

The woman shook her head. 'Her mum died when she was young, her dad's away these two years. They were both alone in life. She was too. I mind the day she left right enough. Her dad took a good drink, so he did, and that day he came back from the pub and sat in his chair talking to all his old army pals who'd come out the skirting-board to say hello to him. Mary left that minute. It was a dark night, heavy rain, she just put on her coat and walked out of the door and we never saw her again. Her dad reported her missing, though.'

'I'm afraid you never will,' said Sussock. 'See her again.'

'Oh.' The woman slumped against the door frame.

'I'm sorry, but we have discovered a body.'

'A body?'

'A skeleton, in fact. We have made a positive identification and it is that of your stepdaughter, Mary Manning.'

'All these years. What has she been doing with herself?'

'I regret that the indications are that she died not long after leaving the house.'

'Not long . . . but she's been gone over twenty years now . . . she'd be a middle-aged woman, married, I thought with a family, she couldn't have stayed on the streets for ever . . .' The woman seemed to sober rapidly. Upstairs a toilet flushed and the semi-naked man padded back across the landing, still over-concentrating, still not apparently aware of the open door and the stranger on the threshold.

'Where did she go?'

'We don't know.'

'How . . .'

'Murdered,' said Sussock. 'She was murdered. Maybe on

the very night she left the house, leaving her dad talking to his army mates.'

'. . . Abernethy,' said Abernethy. 'Or the duty CID officer. Thanks.' He replaced the 'phone. It rang instantly. 'Abernethy,' he said, snatching it up.

'Switchboard, sir. An optician 'phoned. They didn't want to hold until your line cleared. They left their number if you'd like to 'phone them back.'

Abernethy 'phoned them back. Listened. He replaced the 'phone and stared at his notepad.

He had been given a name, and a date of birth.

He had been given an address.

He knew, he knew, he just knew that this was it.

Slowly he picked up the 'phone and dialled a two-figure internal number. 'Collator?' he asked softly when the call was answered.

There was an agitated nervous tap on Donoghue's door. He looked up. Abernethy stood on the threshold holding a dusty file in his hand.

'Come in, Abernethy.'

'I think we've got something here, sir.' He handed Donoghue the file.'

'Oh. Take a seat.' He opened the file. 'Sara Gallagher of Lansdowne Circus—'

'That's—?'

'Just off Great Western Road, sir, opposite Park Road.'

'Got it, yes . . . date of birth . . . that would make her sixty-four . . .' Donoghue looked at the thickness of the file. 'Have you read this?'

'Enough to get the gist of it, sir.'

'Which is?'

'She has a psychiatric history.'

'Uh-huh.'

'She was in the state hospital for some time, a considerable time.'

'Criminally insane.'

'She murdered her two children.' Abernethy shuffled nervously in the chair. 'It makes gruesome reading.'

'Tell me.'

'She smothered them.'

'But it was more than just post-natal depression?'

'Oh yes. They were six and eight years old. There was
some evidence of premeditation in that she cancelled the
eight-year-old's dancing classes—permanently cancelled
them—a few days before she murdered her.'

Donoghue turned a page of the file and glanced up at
Abernethy. 'Heavens,' he said.

'The bit that I found hard to stomach is that the forensic
evidence indicated that there was a time lapse of about a
day between the deaths of the children. The eight-year-old
was smothered first, and she and the six-year-old lived in
the same house as the dead child for twenty-four hours,
then she smothered the younger one. She walked into the
police station, this station in fact, and told them what she
had done. They found one child recently deceased, but the
other stiffened with rigor.'

'My heavens.'

'No evidence that the corpse of the elder child was hidden
from the younger during that time.'

'Oh . . .'

'She went to Carstairs, then to Leverndale. Locked ward,
of course.'

'I should hope so.'

'She was committed at Her Majesty's pleasure when she
was only twenty-four.'

'So she had her first child at sixteen?'

'Yes. Her second at eighteen, to two different fathers

according to the file. Her own family were well off. She murdered her children in her parents' house—'

'The Lansdowne Circus address?'

'Yes, sir. She continued to live with them. It was when they were away for a holiday that she murdered her children. She was deemed sane when she was about forty-three or forty-four and discharged. She went back to the Lansdowne Circus address which by then was hers, having inherited it. Her parents died when she was in hospital.'

'I see. She was then discharged at about forty-five years of age.'

'Yes, sir, but has been admitted and discharged a number of times since then.'

'And if she did murder Mary Manning . . .'

'Who?'

'The skeleton has been identified. Ray Sussock's on his way back from Airdrie where her relatives live.'

'I see.'

'If she did murder her, she did so within a few weeks of being discharged.'

'So much for the medical assessment, sir.'

'Well, judge not that ye be judged, Abernethy. It's the same in every profession. We only hear about the ones they get wrong, not the hundreds of times they get it right. The police are no exception. But if Sara Gallagher is our person we've no idea how many people she has been quietly murdering over the last quarter of a century. How did you get on to her?'

'She suffers double vision and made an appointment to see her optician, having lost her spectacles. The optician in question 'phoned us in response to an earlier request I'd made of him and other opticians to alert us if someone with that condition presented, especially if they needed a replacement pair of spectacles.'

'Good man. This was her discharge address twenty-five years ago?'

'It still is. I checked the voters' roll. She's the only resident.'

'She's not, you know. With a bit of luck Tim Moore is there with her. Who's in the building? Who else besides we two?'

'None in CID, sir.'

'Any female officers?'

WPC Willems.'

'Right. A sergeant and three men, plus WPC Willems, to meet us in the muster room in five minutes.'

'Very good, sir.'

There was a second reverent tap on his door. Ray Sussock stepped over the threshold.

'Don't take your coat off, Ray,' said Donoghue, rising from his seat.

Lansdowne Circus is an enclave of once prestigious houses built in the final years of the nineteenth century for the prosperous middle classes. Now, in the late twentieth century, the homes had for the most part been divided into bedsitters for students, for vulnerable people, the mildly mentally handicapped, the unemployed, the unemployable, the drying out, the coyly termed 'night people'. There were shrubs set in concrete tubs, but the concrete on the buildings was cracked, windows were boarded up and the cars in the street were wrecks.

No. 27 Lansdowne Circus had to Donoghue's eyes what he often termed a shabby-genteel appearance. He noted a solid oak door, sun-bleached and winter-worn. It had a single metal knocker and only one name on the door— Gallagher. Neighbouring doors had up to eight different bells, eight different names on the door, often written on paper and Sellotaped in place. Donoghue's interest in the architecture of his native city allowed him the passing indulgence that once the likely business had been concluded he might, he thought, might be able to view an un-modernized nineteenth-century town house.

Abernethy went up to the door and rapped the knocker, twice, authoritatively. Two uniformed officers stood close behind him. Across the street a woman walking her dog stopped and stared, brazenly.

It was in the event a remarkable capitulation. Sudden. Complete. Unconditional. The door was flung open by a tall and well-built woman with an eye patch, indignant that her door had been knocked on. She had a strong jaw, short hair, masculine features, heavy winter clothes, tweed jacket and skirt, despite the heat. She stood in her doorway in a defensive, questioning posture and then she noticed the uniforms and seemed to Donoghue to absorb the implica-tion. Her posture changed, it seemed to soften, he thought, slacken; her arm fell from the door, her shoulders relaxed, and Donoghue thought she uttered a sound, an 'oh', per-haps. But he thought he might have been mistaken. He was not certain.

The woman continued to stand in the doorway.

'Sara Gallagher?' Abernethy asked, clearly, loudly. The woman did not reply. She stood staring at Abernethy and the policemen behind him and at the police officers behind them, then she looked straight ahead of her but no longer seemed to Donoghue to be seeing anything, as if moving to another world. She turned and walked with small steps back into the gloom of her flat, leaving the door open. Abernethy turned and looked at Donoghue.

'Go in,' Donoghue said to Abernethy and the uniformed sergeant. 'Search the place. There's a little boy in there. Look in every room. If he's not in any of the rooms look in the cupboards and wardrobes. If he's not there, tear up the floorboards.'

The cops entered, bursting into rooms.

Donoghue and Sussock followed the woman, they found her standing in the living-room, vaulted roof and crenellated ceiling, heavy furniture, large velvet curtains only partly opened. She stood facing away from Donoghue and Sussock, facing the fireplace, but still not seeming to see anything.

Donoghue walked up to her. She was as tall as he was, probably taller, probably heavier. He looked into her eyes. They were cold, distant and empty. 'Miss Gallagher?'

No reply.

'She's not with us, Ray.' Donoghue turned to Sussock. 'Don't know where she is, but she's not with us.'

'Sir!' An urgent voice from the hallway.

Donoghue and Sussock went into the hallway. A constable stepped from a walk-in cupboard. A boy in his arms.

'Alive?' Donoghue asked, and then he saw Tim Moore's eyes open. 'Take him to the Children's Hospital, advise them that whatever else they may find we believe him to have been deprived of food and fluid for up to five days.'

'Very good, sir.'

'WPC Willems.'

'Sir?'

'Perhaps you'd like to advise the parents that they can attend at the Sick Kids as soon as they like.'

'Love to, sir.' She smiled and turned.

Donoghue and Sussock returned to the living-room. Sara Gallagher had not moved. 'Sergeant,' Donoghue called softly. There was no longer any urgency.

'Sir?' The sergeant and the constable entered the room.

Donoghue touched Sara Gallagher's arm and turned her gently. She was compliant.

'Take this lady to the station, please, Sergeant. When you get there, ask the police surgeon to attend. Tell him the story and request that she be referred to a psychiatric facility as soon as possible. Don't leave her unattended for a second.'

The sergeant took one arm, the constable the other, and Sara Gallagher was led gently away.

'Well, Ray,' said Donoghue, 'let's see what we've got.'

What they found was a bathtub three-quarters full of water and a packet of salt on the floor beside it. It was just a bathtub full of water but its intended purpose made it offensive to both men. Donoghue stooped and pulled the plug chain and as he did so his fingers touched the surface of the water. It was still warm. He said so.

Sussock caught his breath. 'If we had been ten minutes later . . .'

'Doesn't bear thinking about.'

What they found was a pile of carpet off-cuts, each large enough to conceal a body.

What they found was a bunch of car keys. Perhaps thirty in all.

What they found was Abernethy, pale, drawn, leafing through a photograph album.

'It was on the bedside cabinet,' he said disbelievingly, handing the album to Donoghue. 'Like it was bedtime reading.'

There were twenty-two prints from a Polaroid camera, pictures of eight women, and one of Tim Moore.

'That's Sandra Shapiro.' Donoghue handed the print to Sussock. 'In fact, there are three of her.'

'That's Mary Manning,' said Sussock.

The women were all bound hand and foot with rope. Their expressions ranged from sheer terror to placid resignation.

'They all seem slightly built,' Donoghue noted. 'She would have had no trouble overpowering any of them.'

'Six women to be identified,' said Sussock. 'I dare say six

missing persons files can be closed, and six families' worst fears realized.'

'A neat way for you to round off, Ray.' Donoghue closed the album. 'In at the beginning and twenty-five years on you're in at the end. Not many officers can say that.'

The woman stepped out of the house and into the sun. She carried a bag of clothing, and a handbag containing documents and what cash she had been able to find when she had reached the decision. She walked across the yard, up the track, out of the hollow. She had plenty of time, all the time in the world. He'd told her that he would want his supper late that night, so he did, that meant he'd be coming home with a good drink in him, so he would.

Again.

No more. No, no, no more.

The policemen had treated her differently. Treated her with respect. They had pointed the way forward for her.

She walked, and she felt a weight sliding off her shoulders.

She walked, and she began to smile.

She walked, she noticed the green of the trees and the blue of the sky.

She walked, and she felt a delicious flush of freedom warming her, enveloping her.

Linda McWilliams was leaving her husband.

Linda McWilliams was returning to the city.